NANCY 69

NANCY DREW MYSTER

CAROLYN KEENE

CLUE IN THE
ANCIENT DISGUISE

CLUE IN THE ANCIENT DISGUISE

by
Carolyn Keene

Illustrated by
Paul Frame

WANDERER BOOKS
Published by Simon & Schuster, New York

A Simon & Schuster Division of
Gulf & Western Corporation
Simon & Schuster Building
1230 Avenue of the Americas
New York, New York 10020

Manufactured in the United States of America
10   9   8   7   6   5   4   3   2   1

WANDERER and colophon are trademarks
of Simon & Schuster

NANCY DREW and NANCY DREW MYSTERY STORIES
are trademarks of Stratemeyer Syndicate
registered in the United States Patent
and Trademark Office

Library of Congress Cataloging in Publication Data

Keene, Carolyn.
Clue in the ancient disguise.

(Nancy Drew mystery stories; #69)
Summary: A young Frenchman consults Nancy Drew for help
in unraveling a mystery surrounding his ancestors.
[1. Mystery and detective stories] I. Frame, Paul,
1913-   ill. II. Title. III. Series: Keene, Carolyn.
Nancy Drew mystery stories; no. 69.
PZ7.K23 Nan no. 69   [Fic]   82-15966
ISBN 0-671-45553-2
ISBN 0-671-45552-4 (pbk.)

CONTENTS

1

Alarm Call

"Nancy, my client here needs a mystery solved," said Attorney Carson Drew. "I'm hoping you may be able to help him."

"I'll be glad to try, Dad."

A tall, dark-haired young man bowed and shook hands with Nancy Drew as the lawyer introduced him. "This is Mr. Pierre Michaud... or perhaps I should say *Monsieur* Michaud, since he comes from France."

The young man smiled. "Simply Pierre Michaud will do very well, *merci*."

He was certainly handsome, Nancy observed, with finely chiseled features that included a high-bridged, slightly aquiline nose and strong, dimpled chin. His wide-set, dark eyes were especially striking.

5

"I am told you have a great talent for solving mysteries, Miss Drew," he went on.

The lovely young sleuth, whose red-gold hair and sparkling blue eyes were among her own most striking features, smiled back. "You'd better take nothing for granted until we see if I can help in your case," she chuckled. "Tell me all about it."

The Frenchman explained that as he had no relatives, he had closed his family's small house near the Riviera before coming to America. "While disposing of some of my late grandfather's belongings," Pierre continued, "I came across this letter."

He handed Nancy a folded sheet of blue stationery. To her surprise, it bore an engraved address in her own hometown of River Heights and the name *Louise Duval*. According to the typewritten date in one corner, the letter had been written thirty years ago. It read:

Dear M. Michaud,

While tracing an ancestress of mine, I have made a startling discovery which may be of great importance to both of us.

I prefer to say nothing more until all the facts are clear. But I am planning a trip to France

soon, and I shall look forward to informing you in
person of some exciting news at that time.
                                        Sincerely yours,
                                        Louise Duval

Nancy raised her eyes from the letter in a questioning glance at the young Frenchman. "Do you know if this Duval woman ever did come to visit your grandfather?"

Pierre Michaud responded with a quizzical shrug. "I have no idea. That is why I first consulted your father."

Carson Drew spoke up. "You see, Nancy, that address on the letter no longer exists. Apparently the house was torn down some years ago to make way for an industrial park. So Pierre asked me to try and trace Louise Duval."

"Any luck, Dad?"

"I'm afraid not. From town hall records, I learned that Miss Duval has been dead for many years. She died soon after that letter was written, in fact. However, her will is on file at the county courthouse, and by checking out names from that source, I learned that she has one living descendant, a grandniece named Lisa Thorpe."

Nancy frowned reflectively. "Sounds familiar. I wonder if I've ever met her."

"Quite possibly. Or you may have seen her

name on the society page of the *Record* at some time or other. She's the daughter of a wealthy businessman, Norton Thorpe."

Nancy turned back to Pierre. "And have you talked to Miss Thorpe?"

"*Oui*, I have seen her on several occasions, but she and her father had never even heard of Louise Duval's letter to my grandfather." With a slight flush, the Frenchman added, "Unfortunately Mr. Thorpe was not very kindly. I might even say that he made no secret of disliking me. As a result, neither he nor Lisa was of much help."

From Pierre's tone of voice and the way he referred to Lisa Thorpe by her first name, Nancy suspected that his contact with the Thorpes might have been a good deal more interesting than he let on.

For the moment, however, she decided not to probe further and changed the subject. "If Louise Duval died soon after she wrote to your grandfather," Nancy said, "it sounds as though she never went to France as she intended."

Pierre Michaud nodded. "*Oui*, I think so, too, and therefore nothing came of her letter. No doubt that is why I myself was unaware of it until I discovered it in my grandfather's effects."

Carson Drew glanced at his watch and announced that it was almost noon.

"I've taken the liberty of having my secretary reserve a table at Marco's," he went on. "I thought you two might want to continue your discussion over lunch."

"That would be a great pleasure," Pierre said. He rose to his feet as the vigorous, distinguished-looking Mr. Drew, whose hair was slightly graying at the temples, came out from behind his desk to offer a parting handshake. "Will you not join us, sir?"

"Regretfully, no, I have another appointment I must keep. Besides," Mr. Drew added with a smile, "Nancy will probably elicit all the information she needs much more quickly without any interruptions by me."

Marco's was only a block away from Carson Drew's law office. Nancy liked its comfortable, relaxed atmosphere and red-checked tablecloths. She often ate there with her father when helping him on one of his law cases.

Today the waiter seated her and Pierre by the front window, brought their orders swiftly, and left them to enjoy the delicious Italian food.

"You mentioned that you were already planning to come to America when you ran across Miss Duval's letter," Nancy said after they began eating.

"*Oui*, that is so," Pierre replied.

9

"Are you here mainly on business, then, or just on vacation?"

"On business." The young Frenchman explained that he was an electronics engineer and had come to the United States hoping to interest some American manufacturer in a new type of computer memory which he had invented. "There is still much work to be done in perfecting my device, you see, but that will take money. Luckily, I found a backer soon after I arrived in this country."

"Someone in River Heights?" Nancy inquired.

"No, his name is Mr. Varney. He is a rather quiet financier who dislikes publicity and specializes in developing new products for industry. We met in New York City. But when I told him that I wished to spend some time in River Heights for personal reasons, he very kindly rented a small vacant building here for me to use as my workshop."

"That was certainly a lucky break." Nancy hesitated a moment, then said gently, "I don't mean to pry, but would you care to tell me any more about your talks with Lisa Thorpe and her father? It might give me a lead to follow up in unraveling this case."

Pierre glanced down at his plate with an embarrassed expression. When he looked up and met Nancy's gaze, he smiled regretfully. *"Eh bien*, I may as well be frank, since you have been kind enough to try and help me. The truth is, I found Miss Thorpe very attractive. She seemed to like me, too, and I hoped that we might become better acquainted."

"Norton Thorpe, however, disapproved of his daughter becoming involved with a foreigner who had no job and little money. His manner was quite insulting," Pierre confided. "I am not used to such rudeness, and I refused to be bullied. So he made it clear that I was no longer welcome in his house."

"What about Lisa herself?" asked Nancy.

The young Frenchman shrugged unhappily. "She is very much—how do you say?—under her father's thumb. Indeed, she seems almost afraid of him. So I assume she has bowed to his wishes, and that is why she has not returned my calls."

Their table by the window gave a clear view of the street outside. Nancy was about to go on discussing the Thorpes, when suddenly she frowned.

"Do you see that man standing across the street?" she murmured.

Pierre glanced out the window. "The one in

the doorway of the jewelry shop?"

"Yes." The man was swarthy and, though neatly dressed, was rather tough in appearance, with a heavy jaw and scowling, dark eyebrows.

"Not a very pleasant-looking person," Pierre remarked.

"I agree. Have you ever seen him before?"

"Not that I know of." Pierre glanced at Nancy in surprise. "Why do you ask?"

"Because I noticed him hanging about when we left the building where my father has his office. Now he seems to be watching this restaurant. I'm wondering if he's shadowing us."

Nancy's words brought a frown of concern to Pierre's face. "That is rather worrisome," he said in a grave voice. "My backer, Mr. Varney, warned me to be on the lookout for such a person. Apparently he himself has been annoyed by some troublemaker who bears him a grudge."

Before Nancy could comment, the waiter came bustling toward their table with a phone in one hand. "You have a call from your father's office, Miss Drew!"

She waited until he plugged in the telephone, then lifted the receiver. "This is Nancy."

The voice on the line was that of her father's secretary, Miss Hanson. "I'm sorry to interrupt your lunch, Nancy," she said, "especially with bad news, but this is urgent!"

The young detective listened intently, then thanked Miss Hanson and hung up. Turning to Pierre Michaud, she said, "You have a girl working for you named Nyra Betz?"

"*Oui*, she types and answers the phone and helps out with my experimental work. Why?"

"She just called my father's office to say your workshop is on fire!"

Pierre stood up from the table. "If you will excuse me, Miss Drew, I had better go there at once!"

"Of course. I'll drive you!"

As they hurried out of the restaurant, Nancy noticed that the swarthy watcher was nowhere in sight. Her trim blue sports car was parked in a lot just around the corner. Soon she and Pierre were whizzing through the business district of River Heights.

His workshop was located in a factory district near the railroad tracks on the west side of town. It was a small, two-story brick building that looked as if it might once have housed a repair shop or shipping-company office.

The shrill sound of fire sirens could be heard in the distance as Nancy pulled up in the paved parking area just outside. Billowing smoke and flames were issuing from the building.

As Nancy and the young Frenchman jumped out of her car, a girl's screams rang through the air.

"That is Nyra!" Pierre cried anxiously. "She must be trapped inside!"

2

Faces from the Past

Pierre raced across the pavement to the old wooden door of the building. He shouldered it open and disappeared into the smoke and shooting flames. Nancy held her breath.

Just then the fire engine came thundering up. Raincoated fire fighters jumped off the truck and began connecting a hose to the nearest hydrant.

In a moment, Nancy saw Pierre stagger out of the building, carrying a girl in his arms. She was clinging to his neck, coughing and sobbing hysterically. Nancy and a young fireman rushed forward to help. The girl seemed vexed at the sight of Nancy, but allowed the fireman to help Pierre lower her to the grassy verge of the parking area. She seemed delighted at their concern and attention.

Gradually, after struggling for breath and fluttering her eyelids as if reviving from a faint, she permitted Pierre to help her sit up. Then, in another few moments, with his arm around her, she managed to rise to her feet, but leaned closely against him for support. She was a tall, thin girl with mouse-colored brown hair, and she was not very attractive due to her petulant expression.

Her pale gray eyes focused on the young Frenchman's face as she quavered, "Oh, Pierre! I just left to go down to Center Street to get a bite of lunch. I wasn't gone more than twenty minutes. And I come back to this!"

Pressing her hand to her eyes, she wailed, "Oh, I should never have gone! I hope none of your work is ruined!"

"Now, now," Pierre said, "you are not to worry. You are safe. That is the most important thing."

"No, oh no! Your work is the most important thing. If only you hadn't gone out this morning, all this might never have happened!" she declared, shooting a withering glance at Nancy between sobs. "Whatever else you had to do, surely it didn't matter as much as your work and experiments here!"

Ignoring her comments, Pierre said, "Nancy, let me introduce Nyra Betz, my secretary and all-round helper. She is invaluable!"

Nyra simpered and blushed.

"Hi." The titian-haired girl smiled.

At that moment, Nancy suddenly realized how surprising it was that she and Pierre had reached the scene even before the fire engine arrived. Nyra must have called Carson Drew's office before she even phoned in an alarm! And why hadn't she left the building sooner? Obviously she adored Pierre. Could she have set the blaze herself just for the sake of being rescued by the handsome Frenchman?

Aloud, feeling somewhat sorry for Nyra, Nancy said, "Pierre, you're very lucky to have found someone so capable and dedicated."

The mousy-haired girl glanced at Nancy with less animosity now.

Pierre smiled. "Yes, truly. Nyra and I met when I first went to see the Thorpes, just after I arrived in River Heights. She is a good friend of Lisa's."

Not any more, I'll bet! thought Nancy.

"Later Nyra came to see my workshop," Pierre went on. "When I showed her my memory device and explained how I worked, she volunteered to help me."

"Gee, that was nice of you, Nyra," Nancy said politely.

Meanwhile, the fire fighters had been playing streams of water on the burning building and soon extinguished the small smoky fire.

The fire captain frowned suspiciously as he went inside to inspect the damage. When he came out again, he said to Pierre, "Are you the sole occupant of this building?"

"Yes, I live above my workshop," Pierre replied.

"Any enemies?"

The Frenchman shrugged in surprise. "Not so far as I am aware. Why?"

"Better come in and take a look at this."

Pierre accompanied the fire captain into the building. Nyra and Nancy followed them into the damp, smoke-blackened room.

It was impossible to miss! Across one wall in red spray paint was the ugly threat:

GO HOME, FRENCHY, OR A LOT WORSE WILL HAPPEN!

Nancy felt a shiver of alarm. If she was going to help Pierre, she had better begin her investigation as soon as possible. But where to start on the case? The more she thought about it, the more it seemed that Lisa Thorpe might be the person best able to supply a clue to the mystery.

After excusing herself and saying goodbye, Nancy left Pierre and Nyra still talking to the fire captain, and drove off.

As she rode along with her hands on the

wheel and her eyes on the road, she continued turning the problem over in her head. And suddenly she realized why Lisa Thorpe's name had sounded so familiar when Pierre first mentioned it.

Of course! She worked at the River Heights Thrift Shop with Bess Marvin, one of Nancy's closest friends.

The shop sold clothing donated or gathered by members of a local charitable organization. Nancy glanced at her wristwatch. The shop was open only at certain hours, but someone might be there now.

Coming to a public telephone booth, Nancy swung over to the curb and got out, then looked up the thrift shop number and dialed.

Luckily, her good friend Bess Marvin, answered. She was delighted to hear from Nancy, who said, "Bess, by any chance is Lisa Thorpe working there with you this afternoon? But don't let on that I'm asking about her, please!"

"Oh . . . okay, Nancy, I understand. And the answer is yes."

"Bess, I'd like to meet her, so I'm going to drop by."

Her friend immediately sensed that the famous young detective was hot on the trail of another mystery. "Fabulous! But we're closing for the day in about twenty minutes, Nancy, so you'd better hurry."

"I'm on my way, Bess! See you soon."

Nancy drove to the other side of town. The thrift shop was located two blocks off Main Street, on the first floor of an old house. A bell tinkled as Nancy opened the door and walked in.

Bess and a pretty, laughing girl were tidying the racks of clothing and displays of other donated goods. Bess, who was blond and plump, introduced Lisa, and Nancy could well understand Pierre's interest in her. She had glowing brown eyes and beautiful ivory skin that seemed even more perfect by contrast with her brunette hair. She was perhaps four years older than Nancy and Bess.

Nancy said, "Bess, I was out on an errand, so I thought I'd drop by to persuade you to have a sundae with me."

"Oooh, my weakness! Well, we're almost through here." She turned to Lisa. "Why don't you come along with us?"

"Well, I, . . ." Lisa hesitated.

"That's a splendid idea. Do come," Nancy seconded the invitation. "Let's go to Jake's Ice Cream Parlor. He makes the most delicious hot fudge sundaes!"

So the thrift shop was locked, and the three girls piled into Nancy's car. Soon they were seated in a booth at Jake's. After they had given their orders, Nancy said, "Lisa, I'm so glad you were able to come with us. You see, I've been asked to help Pierre Michaud solve the mystery of Louise Duval's letter to his grandfather."

At the mention of Pierre's name, Nancy noticed that Lisa colored and dropped her eyes.

"Oh yes, he did come to see us about that," she said, looking up again at Nancy. "My father and I had never heard of it before. Louise Duval was my great-aunt, but she's been dead many, many years."

"Oh, this sounds exciting. Tell me about it," Bess said. To Lisa, she added, "Nancy has a reputation for solving mysteries. She's really good."

"Oh, now, Bess." Nancy laughed. But Lisa was looking at her with fresh interest.

"I'd like to help, Nancy. Will you let me?"

"Of course. You can help a great deal. You know that Pierre Michaud found the letter from your great-aunt among his grandfather's effects."

Lisa nodded as she took a spoonful of sundae. "Yes, he said that she mentioned some ancestress in the letter."

"Have you any idea whom she meant?" said Bess.

"Well, I've been thinking about that, and I feel sure it must have been Yvette Duval."

"Pretty name," Bess murmured.

"Yes, and she herself was beautiful. She was French, as you've probably guessed from her name, and she came to this country with her husband about two hundred years ago. They settled right here in River Heights."

"Hm," Nancy said. "What else do you know about her?"

"Not much." Lisa smiled. "As a matter of fact, it's been sort of a tradition in our family that there was something mysterious about Yvette Duval. Something to do with her past, which she never revealed and would never talk about."

"Gee, just the way you say that almost gives me goose bumps!" Bess declared in an awed voice.

The girls were silent for a time, enjoying their sundaes and thinking about Lisa's unusual ancestress.

Breaking the silence, Lisa said hesitantly, "Have you seen Pierre recently?"

Nancy said, "Yes, just today. There was a mysterious fire at his workshop. Nyra Betz discovered it."

"Nyra?" Lisa echoed in surprise. "How did that happen?"

"She works for him now," Nancy said gently. From the expression that flickered briefly on Lisa's face and the way her fingers clenched on the napkin she was holding, Nancy could see that the news had come as a somewhat unpleasant shock to her.

But the brunette girl soon recovered her poise and said, "When Pierre came to see us, I'm afraid my father was quite rude to him. I felt terrible about it. After all, he was a total stranger in this country and had come to us for help or information." Lisa swallowed hard and looked down at the tablecloth.

Always the romantic, Bess shot a significant glance at Nancy and nodded her head sagely.

Soon afterward, Lisa noticed the time. "Golly, I'd better be going. I have to get my car at the thrift shop."

"Don't worry, I'll drive you back," said Nancy.

"Well, thanks. By the way, we have a portrait of Yvette Duval and her husband at my house. Would you like to see it?"

"Oh, yes! Let's, Nancy," said Bess.

On their way to the thrift shop, Lisa pointed

to a big industrial park. "That's where Louise Duval used to live. All that property was hers."

"Wow," said Bess. "Must've been a big place!"

"Yes, and old too. My mother told me all about it. Louise Duval was her aunt, my maternal grandfather's sister."

"Did she live there by herself?" asked Nancy.

"No, she had a maid whom I remember quite well. She used to come and visit us sometimes, even long after Great-Aunt Louise died."

The titian-haired detective was keenly interested in hearing this. "Is her maid still alive?"

Lisa nodded. "Yes, in fact we had a card from her last Christmas. I'll give you her address. Her name's Emily Owsler."

As they were about to turn into the parking lot next to the thrift shop, Nancy gasped. She had just caught sight of the swarthy man who had been watching her and Pierre at Marco's. He was sitting in a car parked near the shop, but now, as if realizing he had been seen, he slowly drove away. Nancy decided she had better tell her dad about him that night.

Lisa got into her own car. Then Nancy and Bess followed her to the Thorpes' house. It was a white, three-story frame mansion with a tower. A spacious porch ran across the front and side of the house.

"It's way too big for us, especially since Mother died," Lisa remarked, "but my father's family has always lived here."

The interior was beautifully furnished. Lisa led them to a paneled hallway with a large, sunny room at one end, full of plants and flowers and white wicker furniture. The portrait she had mentioned hung in the hallway near this room. In addition to the light flooding in through the sunroom, Lisa flicked a switch above the frame which totally illuminated the oil painting.

"This is Yvette and her husband, Paul Duval."

Yvette was a white-skinned beauty with lustrous black curls and flashing dark eyes, dressed in a low-necked gown of the period. Paul Duval, in a dark blue coat and white neck cloth, seemed more stodgy and matter-of-fact, a typical man of business. It was his wife who drew the girls' eyes.

"Gee, she was beautiful," said Bess.

Nevertheless, Nancy sensed a haunting sadness about Yvette's expression.

"I've always imagined her as some sort of adventuress," Lisa remarked.

"Maybe a spy," Nancy suggested half humorously. "After all, the years around 1800 were a time of war in France and Europe."

"Oh yes, that's even more exciting!" Lisa agreed, and so did Bess.

Just then, Nancy heard a door open and shut somewhere in the front of the house, and Lisa suddenly became quiet. Presently a big, heavily built man with brush-cut, graying hair came into the hallway. He was carrying a briefcase.

"Hello, Daddy," Lisa said nervously and introduced him to her two companions.

"Hmph. Afternoon, girls," Norton Thorpe responded curtly. His manner was intimidating.

"Nancy has been asked to help Pierre Michaud discover what Great-Aunt Duval's letter was all about," Lisa went on.

Her words brought an angry flush to Mr. Thorpe's face. His bristling brows came down in a furious scowl. "I thought I told you not to concern yourself any more with that fortune-hunting Frenchman, Lisa!" he thundered.

Turning to Nancy and Bess, he added, "That means none of his investigators or go-betweens are welcome here. I must ask you to leave my house immediately!"

3

Red Juggernaut

There was a moment of stunned, awkward silence. Then Nancy said coolly, "We came here as your daughter's guests, Mr. Thorpe. We naturally assumed this was her home as well as yours, and therefore you would respect her right to invite us. However, if you have different standards and our presence offends you, we certainly won't remain."

Turning to her friend, Nancy said, "Shall we go, Bess?"

Her companion, pink-faced with embarrassment and slightly breathless, exclaimed, "Oh, yes!"

The two girls walked out with their heads high. Norton Thorpe, who evidently was not used to being defied or spoken to in this fashion, looked on, fuming with anger. From his flushed, tight-lipped expression, he seemed at a loss for the right words to put this impudent young female, Nancy Drew, in her place.

Lisa watched what was happening with a pale, frightened face. She seemed to have been shocked into silence by her father's harsh outburst.

Nevertheless, she hurried after her two guests and murmured, "I'm awfully sorry about this!"

Nancy squeezed her hand and gave her a reassuring smile. "Don't be upset, Lisa. We understand. It wasn't your fault."

Outside, as the two girls reached Nancy's car, Bess Marvin let out an indignant gasp. "Of all the rude people! That man is impossible!"

Nancy generously was ready to make allowances. "Perhaps he had a hard day at the office."

"He certainly must be difficult to live with!" Bess declared as she climbed in beside the pretty young sleuth. "No wonder Lisa didn't return Pierre's calls. She's probably scared to death of her father."

"Pierre said she was under his thumb. When you stop to think of it, it was brave of her to come apologize in front of him, as she did."

"Mr. Thorpe's so overbearing, I'll bet she's never seen anyone stand up to him. Maybe your example helped to put a little backbone into her, Nancy."

Nancy found it hard not to smile, remembering Bess's own timid, soft-hearted ways. All the same, from several of their past adventures, she knew that her friend could be as brave as anyone in a real emergency.

"If you're right, Bess, then I'm glad it happened," Nancy said aloud. "Also, I learned one thing from our visit to Lisa's that could be very helpful."

"What's that?"

"How to get in touch with Louise Duval's former maid."

After dropping her girl friend off at the Marvins', Nancy returned home. As she walked in the door, Hannah Gruen said, "You had a phone call while you were out, dear."

The kindly, middle-aged woman had been the Drew's housekeeper ever since the attorney's wife had passed away when Nancy was a little girl.

"Who was it, Hannah?"

"The curator of the art museum. Mr. Gregory, I think he said his name was. He'd like you to help investigate those two break-ins we heard about on the news."

Nancy's eyes sparkled with interest. "Sounds exciting!"

"But not dangerous, I hope," said the motherly housekeeper, her voice taking on a note of concern.

"Don't worry, Hannah," the young detective chuckled. "I doubt that the case will be all *that* exciting. But I'll be careful!"

After looking up Emily Owsler's number in the telephone directory, Nancy called the former maid. An elderly voice answered. Nancy explained that she was looking into a matter that concerned the maid's former mistress and asked if she might drop by for a visit at some convenient time.

"Why of course, Miss Drew. I'll be home all evening, if you care to stop in."

"Thank you, that would be nice."

After helping Hannah with the dinner dishes, Nancy started out in her car about 8:30. It was a chill autumn night with a gathering mist that filmed her windshield with moisture.

Emily Owsler's address turned out to be a modest apartment building on the outskirts of River Heights. The person who opened the door was a slender, gray-haired woman in her seventies.

"Please come in, Miss Drew. I've read in the paper about some of the mysteries you've solved."

The ex-maid seemed eager to chat, and

Nancy had no trouble steering the conversation around to the subject of her former employer. But Miss Owsler had no idea why Louise Duval might have written to Pierre's grandfather, even though Nancy could supply the exact date of the letter.

"I remember the time very well, though," Emily Owsler mused sadly. "It was just a few weeks later that Miss Duval died."

"Can you think of anything at all unusual that might have happened around that time?" Nancy probed.

Miss Owsler knit her brow. "Hm, I do recall her hiring a person to do some special work for her that summer. I think 'foreign research' was the way she referred to it."

"But you don't remember who that person was?"

"Not really. Some sort of expert, I believe, but I couldn't say what he was an expert in, or exactly what she hired him to do. Come to think of it, it was a secret . . ."

The woman's face suddenly brightened as she went on, "Yes, I do recall now! Miss Louise was quite excited about the whole thing. And I remember how she sounded when she mentioned it to some of her friends—as if she was just bursting to tell them some exciting news, but had to wait for the right time, after this research—or whatever it was—was completed."

All this, Nancy thought, sounded very much like the tone of Louise Duval's mysterious letter to Pierre's grandfather ... which, in turn, convinced her that the so-called 'research' might hold the key to the mystery.

"You know, Miss Drew," Emily Owsler continued, "you might be able to find out more from Miss Louise's lawyer."

"That sounds like a good idea. Can you tell me his name?"

"Yes, Jonas Becker. And his law firm is Hylig & Becker. I know because they're the ones I get my monthly pension check from."

Nancy thanked the woman for her information. Then she said, "In that letter I told you about, Miss Duval wrote that she was planning to go to France. But apparently she never did, nor followed up her letter in any way. I assume that's because she died rather suddenly and unexpectedly."

Emily Owsler nodded, her face clouding at the memory. "Yes, that's right. Miss Louise died of a heart attack after a very unpleasant experience."

"Oh? What was that?" asked Nancy, her detective instincts immediately aroused.

"Well, you see, she was out for a stroll one

evening. She always liked to go for a walk after dinner, said it was good for her digestion. Anyhow, she came rushing in soon afterward—all upset and out of breath, clutching her bosom. I asked her what was wrong, and she said a big red car had almost run her down!"

Miss Owsler dabbed her eyes with a handkerchief, obviously distressed as the circumstances of her mistress's death came back to her. "I phoned her doctor right away and gave her two of the pills he'd prescribed, and then made her a cup of tea," she went on, "but the poor soul died just a few minutes later, before the doctor could arrive. We'd all known for some time, of course, that she had a weak heart."

The ex-maid gulped back tears and blew her nose.

"I'm sorry to bring back these sad memories," Nancy apologized. "It must be very upsetting to talk about."

"That's all right, my dear. I'm glad if what I've told you has been of any help."

Nancy thanked Miss Owsler and made her way downstairs in the apartment elevator. Outside the building, the night mist was thickening, and the streetlights glowed in the darkness with a foggy halo. Nancy turned on her windshield wipers after starting the car.

She had gone only a couple of blocks when

she noticed a car coming up behind her in the rear-view mirror. Its headlights were off, which made the outlines of the car easier to discern. Despite the mist, the street lamps shed enough light for Nancy to see that the car was red.

But she could make out no one at the wheel!

Nancy's heart gave a lurch. This fog must be playing tricks with my eyes! she thought.

Nervously she swung over to the right, to give the car behind her room to pass. But it made no attempt to do so. And when she speeded up, it too increased speed so as to stay little more than a couple of car lengths behind her!

Nancy's pulse was beating fearfully now. "That can't be a ghost car!" she told herself. "It must have a driver, even if I can't see him!"

But why was he trailing her? Was he just waiting for the right moment to pounce in some way?

Nancy clenched her teeth and tried to keep calm. There was always the hope that she might sight a police cruiser, and anyhow she hadn't much farther to go.

Meanwhile, the reddish car continued to follow her through the misty darkness! Although the visibility was too poor to tell its make or year, Nancy had the impression that it was large and old-fashioned!

When at last she came to her own corner, she

swung the wheel violently, then stared in the rear-view mirror. To her relief, the other car had sped on past the intersection and was no longer following her.

Nancy's heart was still pumping furiously when she stopped and switched off the ignition moments later. Leaving her car parked in the driveway, she jumped out, eager to get inside the house. But before she could mount the front steps, she received another shock.

A sinister figure detached itself from the shadows of the shrubbery and came striding toward her. *Once again, it was the swarthy, tough-looking man whom she and Pierre had glimpsed out the restaurant window!*

4

Car Snoop

"Wait! Do not try to run inside!" The man spoke with a heavy foreign accent, his voice laden with menace. "I have come to talk to you!"

Nancy caught her breath, but struggled to keep her own voice calm as she replied, "This is a strange time and a strange way to start a conversation."

Summoning up her courage, she went on boldly, "Who are you, and why have you been following me around, spying on me?"

"Never mind all that!" the dark-visaged stranger growled. "I am the one who will ask the questions. And you will answer. Are you a friend of Pierre Michaud's?"

"Yes, I know him, if that's what you mean, and I consider him a friend. He has asked me to

37

investigate something that happened a long time ago."

"Well, you had better drop the job right now and stop helping him in any way, or you will find yourself in serious trouble! Do you understand?"

Nancy shrank back as his brutal face glared at her out of the semi-darkness.

"And now you will tell me something more. Where did you go tonight, and whom was it you saw?" When she hesitated, he took a step toward her.

Nancy felt a fresh pang of alarm but said in a defiant voice, "What I do or whom I see is none of your business! You'd better stop bothering me or I'll call the police!"

The man shook his fist threateningly. "I am warning you, girl! You had better not—"

He had raised his voice to scare Nancy, but now he suddenly broke off as he noticed a movement at the window out of the corner of his eye. The curtains twitched and shrill barking followed as Nancy's pet bull terrier, Togo, looked out and decided to arouse the Drew household. He sensed that his beloved young mistress was in danger.

Nancy silently blessed the faithful, alert little dog because his barking had clearly unnerved her sinister caller. The man began to back away, still shaking his fist and muttering, "Remember what I have said!"

A moment later, the porch light came on and the scowling stranger ran off into the darkness. Hannah Gruen opened the front door as the young sleuth hurried up the porch steps.

"Nancy! Is something wrong?" the housekeeper exclaimed. "Why was Togo barking?"

"There was someone out there, Hannah. But don't worry, he's gone now."

Nancy flung herself down gratefully in an easy chair in the bright, comfortable living room. With a sigh of relief, she ran her fingers through her hair.

"I'll bet you're mighty glad to get home on a night like this," Hannah murmured sympathetically.

"Oh, you have no idea how glad! I had quite a fright tonight, coming home."

"What happened, dear?"

"A car followed me—a big, old-fashioned-looking red car. Its lights were off, for one thing, but the really scary part was that it looked as if it had no driver!"

The housekeeper gasped. "Are you serious, Nancy?"

"You bet I am! Oh, I realize my eyes were probably playing tricks on me, what with the mist and all, but that's how it looked."

Hannah shook her head in amazement. "My goodness, that's enough to give anyone a fright."

"What made it even worse," Nancy continued, "was that the person I visited tonight had just been telling me how a woman was frightened to death thirty years ago by a red car that almost ran her down."

The housekeeper shuddered slightly and clucked her tongue. "No wonder you were upset. That's really spooky, even if the whole thing was just a coincidence—and it surely must have been, Nancy, don't you think so?"

"You're probably right, Hannah. But that wasn't all. Just as I got home and started to go up on the porch, a tough-looking man stepped out of the shrubbery. He tried to scare me off a case I'm investigating for Dad."

Hannah was shocked and outraged by this news. "Shouldn't we call the police?" she urged.

"I'm afraid it wouldn't do much good," Nancy replied. "Even if I'd phoned the moment I got in the house, he'd probably have been long gone by the time a scout car got here. I imagine he had a car parked up the street or around the corner."

"Poor dear, you've really had an awful night of it!" The housekeeper leaned down to give

Nancy a comforting hug and added, "You be sure and tell your father all this when he gets home, and see what he says."

"That's exactly what I intend to do."

"Good! In the meantime, I'm going to make you a nice cup of tea."

"Oh, would you, Hannah? That'd be lovely!"

Nancy felt a great deal better, now that she had unburdened herself to the motherly housekeeper. Hannah Gruen's sturdy common sense always helped to put even the eeriest mystery into the proper perspective.

She was prepared to stay up and keep Nancy company until Mr. Drew returned, but the teenage detective would not hear of it. "No, no! You go to bed, Hannah," she insisted. "Isn't tomorrow your day at the hospital?"

"Yes, it is. So perhaps I will, Nancy, if you don't mind," Hannah said, stifling a yawn. She had volunteered to work at the River Heights Hospital one day a week.

After Hannah had gone upstairs, Nancy sat pondering the unpleasant encounter that had taken place when she arrived home. I wonder who that fellow is, she mused.

The swarthy man had spoken with a French accent. Could he be Pierre's enemy, the one who set the workshop fire and wrote the warning on the wall? . . . But no, that hardly seemed possible. They had seen him outside the restaurant just before Nancy got the call about the fire, so how could he be in two places at once?

Presently she heard her father's key turning in the lock and went to greet him.

"Well, this is a pleasant surprise." He smiled wearily and kissed Nancy. "But how come you left your car in the drive, dear? I hope you aren't planning to go out again this late, because I've already put it away."

"No, that's fine, Dad. Thanks for attending to it. I'm sorry I left you that extra chore," Nancy apologized. "I meant to do it myself but forgot. You see, I had a rather unpleasant experience tonight . . ."

She broke off suddenly with a rueful grin. "But never mind that now, I'll explain later. First, come on in the kitchen, Dad, and let me make you a sandwich and a cup of tea."

"Just the tea, thanks, Nancy." Carson Drew patted her fondly on the shoulder. "I had a late working dinner with a client."

In a few minutes the tea was ready. As they sat sipping it at the kitchen table, Nancy told her father about the day's mysterious developments. Like Hannah, he was greatly concerned about the swarthy stranger who had lurked outside the house in order to question Nancy. Mr. Drew said he would personally report the incident to Police Chief McGinnis next morning.

"Thanks, Dad. And by the way," Nancy continued, "I have a new clue to follow up in Pierre Michaud's case. The maid I was just telling you about, Emily Owsler, said that Louise Duval's lawyer was Jonas Becker, of Hylig & Becker. Do you know him?"

"I did, Nancy, but I'm sorry to say both he and Mr. Hylig are dead. The firm is now run by one of their former law clerks, a fellow by the name of Maxwell Fleen."

Nancy was disappointed. She explained that she had been hoping Jonas Becker could supply the name of the expert Miss Duval had hired long ago to carry out the foreign research she needed. "But maybe Mr. Fleen can help me."

Carson Drew shook his head dubiously. "Fleen's not a very accommodating fellow. I've always had a feeling that . . . well, that he's not quite on the up and up."

Nancy frowned uncertainly, knowing how reluctant her father was to cast aspersions on another member of his profession without good reason. "Care to be any more specific, Dad?"

Mr. Drew shrugged. "Let's just say I get the impression there's something about his character or actions that wouldn't stand too close scrutiny. Anyway, I'm not on a friendly footing with him."

"Thanks for warning me, Dad. I'll bear that in mind."

Next morning, on her way to the art museum, Nancy stopped in the offices of Hylig & Becker. The receptionist, a stout, heavily made-up woman, sniffed in disapproval on hearing that Nancy had no appointment.

"Kindly have a chair. I'll see if Mr. Fleen can spare you a moment."

The atmosphere did not improve when Nancy was finally ushered into Maxwell Fleen's inner sanctum. He was a narrow-faced, pinched-lipped man, sallow and scowling. After hearing her request, Fleen shook his head curtly. "Absolutely not."

"But Miss Duval has been dead for thirty years," Nancy pointed out. "Could it do any possible harm now to answer my question?"

"Miss Drew," Fleen said coldly, "three years, thirty years, it makes no difference. I would never discuss my client's affairs with an outsider."

Disappointed, Nancy left the fourth-floor suite of offices and went back down to the street, where she had parked. She smiled in surprise as she saw Bess Marvin and Bess's cousin, George Fayne, standing by her car.

"Well! Small world. What are you two doing here?"

George, a slim girl with short, dark hair, said, "This *is* your car, isn't it, Nancy?"

"Of course. Don't you recognize it?"

"Just wanted to make sure," George explained. "We caught someone snooping inside it a few minutes ago."

"We don't know what she was doing," Bess added indignantly, "but she had her head and arms inside the window."

"Who did?" Nancy asked, startled and mystified.

"A tall, skinny girl with sort of light brown hair. But don't ask us who she was. She didn't wait around to answer any questions."

"I think she saw us coming in the rear-view mirror," George went on. "When Bess and I started hurrying toward the car, she ran off."

"Hm." Nancy considered for a moment. "I guess there's nothing too bad she could do just leaning in the window . . . unless she was trying to steal something out of the glove compartment. Let me check."

To Nancy's relief, the glove compartment was still locked. "Oh well, no harm done, I guess. Just another mystery to add to my collection. Are you two out shopping, by the way?"

"We were," Bess said. "George just bought a new pair of shoes. Why?"

"Care to come to the art museum with me?"

"Sure, sounds like a fun idea!" George spoke up enthusiastically. Bess agreed.

Five minutes later, they arrived at the imposing, Greek-pillared museum that was set in a lovely green park. But as they walked into the lobby, an alarm bell suddenly began ringing loudly!

5

Weird Intruders

A buzz of excitement filled the museum. Visitors milled about, staring in all directions. Some turned to query the nearest guard or attendant, but the museum employees seemed as startled as everyone else.

"What's happening, Nancy?" Bess exclaimed.

"I've no idea," her friend admitted with a helpless shrug.

As suddenly as it had begun, the alarm bell stopped ringing. As the echoes died away, a calming voice spoke over the public-address system. "Ladies and gentlemen, this is the curator speaking. There is no need to leave the building, so please do not be alarmed. What you have just heard was a mistake—repeat, a *mistake*. The alarm bell went off accidentally. We regret any inconvenience this may have caused, and we hope you will go on enjoying your public art museum as if nothing has happened. Thank you."

"Whew! That's a relief," said George.

Nancy smiled and agreed, then asked, "Do you two want to look around while I go talk to the curator?"

"Okay," Bess said eagerly. "We'll start in the Medieval and Renaissance rooms over there, and work our way around to Modern."

Nancy went up a broad, marble staircase that arose from the center hall of the museum. On the second floor, she made her way to a suite of offices at the rear of the building.

The balding, elderly curator, Mr. Gregory, rose from his desk to greet her as his secretary announced the pretty young sleuth.

"Nancy, how good of you to stop in! It's a pleasure to see you!"

"I certainly arrived at an exciting moment," Nancy chuckled.

Mr. Gregory smiled ruefully. "Repairmen are testing and reconnecting the alarm system, which is how it happened to go off. So in a way it's related to your coming here this morning."

He invited her to have a chair and added, "How much do you know about our break-ins?"

"Only the bare facts," Nancy replied. "There have been two, haven't there?"

"Yes, and the curious thing is that nothing was taken on either occasion."

"That *is* odd," Nancy mused. "Are you sure they weren't just pranks?"

"Quite sure. The first time, our night watchman was violently attacked, and the same thing almost happened during the second break-in."

"Please tell me about them, Mr. Gregory."

The curator explained that, on the first occasion, the intruders were believed to have hidden in the public rest room just before closing time. This was indicated by cigarette ashes and a chewing-gum wrapper which were found on the tiled floor next morning, even though the rest room had been cleaned by a janitor at the end of the previous day.

"Later, after the staff had left, the intruders emerged and overpowered the night watchman. They left him tied and gagged."

"Do you have any idea what they did, or where they went, after tying up the watchman?" Nancy asked.

"At least part of the time they were in the basement storage area. We know that definitely, because things had been moved around."

Mr. Gregory said that because of the first break-in, he had alerted guards to search all restrooms extra carefully just before closing time.

Perhaps because of this precaution, the intruders resorted to other means for their second break-in.

"The alarm system was tampered with. Police Chief McGinnis said it looked like the work of professional burglars."

"But again nothing was taken?" put in Nancy.

"Not as far as we could determine. However, soon after midnight, the watchman thought he heard noises in the basement. When he entered the storage area to investigate, a stack of crates toppled over. He could have been badly hurt. As it was, he suffered a bruised and sprained shoulder. We think the accident was contrived, and that the intruders escaped while this was happening."

As Nancy pondered what Mr. Gregory had just told her, she noticed a large, framed photograph hanging near his desk. It showed several people standing on the front steps of the museum. From their old-fashioned clothing and the slight fading and yellowing of the picture, it appeared to have been taken many years ago.

A hand-lettered inscription at the bottom of the photograph read: *Curator and Members of the Duval Family at the Opening of the River Heights Art Museum, 1893.*

"The Duval family!" Nancy exclaimed in surprise. "Are they connected with this museum in some way?"

"Oh yes, indeed. They donated a great deal of money to help build it. In fact, they were moving spirits in founding the museum."

Nancy could not help being struck by the odd coincidence—that just when she was investigating a mysterious letter written by one of the Duvals, unexplained break-ins should occur at a museum endowed by the same family.

Or was it no more than that, a mere coincidence?

"Tell me, Mr. Gregory," Nancy asked on a sudden impulse, "do you know anything about a Miss Louise Duval?"

"Louise Duval?" The curator frowned for a moment, then settled back in his chair with a reminiscent smile. "Yes, as a matter of fact I do. She's dead now, of course, but when I first came to work here, I recall the man who was then chief curator telling me about a tiff he'd had with the old lady."

Mr. Gregory related that when the River Heights Art Museum had first opened, the Duval family had contributed an oil painting as a starter item for the museum's collection.

"The painting was authentically old, mind

you, but of no great artistic value. It hung in the museum throughout the first half of this century, but was finally banished to a storeroom along with other less important art works that we have no room to display. Unfortunately, Miss Duval became incensed when she heard this."

"What happened?" Nancy inquired keenly.

Mr. Gregory shrugged. "She protested very emphatically, but the curator stood firm. He told me that he thought she intended to consult some outside art expert and try to prove that the painting was important enough to keep on display. But she died later that fall, I'm sorry to say, so nothing more was heard on the subject."

Nancy was intrigued. If Miss Duval had passed away soon afterward, this meant that the incident Mr. Gregory described must have taken place the same year that she wrote her mysterious letter to Pierre's grandfather.

And perhaps the painting he referred to was the subject of the research that Miss Duval's maid had mentioned!

"Would it be possible to see that painting, Mr. Gregory?" Nancy asked. "It may be connected with another case I'm working on."

"Of course. But I'm afraid it may take a while to locate it. I'll have one of my staff check it out and let you know when you can view it."

Nancy thanked the curator and promised to apply her detective skills to the mystery of the puzzling break-ins.

When she returned to the main floor of the museum, she found Bess and George talking to a handsome young man in the room where modern works of art were displayed.

"This is Lee Talbot, Nancy," said George Fayne.

"He won first prize at the Riverview Art Show!" Bess added enthusiastically.

"Oh yes, I heard about that." Nancy smiled as he shook her hand. "Congratulations!"

"Thanks. Too bad you girls weren't there to see the award ceremony."

The young man was tall, slim, and casually yet trendily dressed in a cable-knit Irish fisherman's sweater and designer jeans. From her breathless manner and the admiring way her eyes dwelt on him, Bess was clearly very much aware of Lee Talbot's wavy-haired good looks. And he, in turn, seemed to enjoy being the center of attention.

"Was it a painting that won the prize?" Nancy asked him politely.

"Yes, I called it *Feline Still Life.*"

"A memorable composition," said a mocking voice on Nancy's left.

She and her companions turned and saw a

red-haired man in a corduroy jacket, sport shirt, and slacks. Nancy recognized him as Peter Worden, a reporter who wrote on entertainment and art events for the River Heights *Record*. He had spoken rather sarcastically, and Lee Talbot responded with an angry scowl.

"Nobody asked your opinion, Worden!"

"I'm not surprised. You know how I feel about overdoing a subject," the reporter said coolly. "Looking around for fresh material, are you?"

At this remark, Lee Talbot's face flamed with rage. He doubled up his fists and lunged at the reporter!

6

Copycat

Nancy held her breath, wondering what would happen next.

As the artist came toward him, snarling "Why you—!" Peter Worden stood his ground, refusing to flinch or back away. He may or may not have expected Lee Talbot to punch him, but he certainly showed no sign of fear. In fact, he looked so confident and prepared for the attack that perhaps he caused the young artist to think twice about starting a fight.

Whatever the reason, Talbot's hands slowly unclenched and he seemed to bottle up his anger. Turning to the three girls, he apologized curtly. "Sorry. I certainly don't want to embarrass you by causing an ugly scene, but I don't think I can stand the air pollution around here any longer. 'Bye for now, girls!"

Jamming his hands in his jeans as if to keep

them from turning violent against his will, the artist stalked off toward the museum lobby, still flushed and fuming.

Nancy and her two friends stared after his retreating figure and then turned, one by one, to look at Peter Worden.

Bess said, "What on earth was that all about?"

The newsman grinned sheepishly. "Guess I owe you girls an apology, too, for interrupting your chat. I shouldn't have said what I did to Talbot."

George, still puzzled, said, "But what made him so angry?"

Worden shrugged. "It's a long story. I'm a-fraid his prize painting reminded me too much of a picture I'd seen here in the museum. And I made the mistake of hinting as much."

Bess looked indignant. "Why, that's practically saying that he copied!" She clearly felt protective toward the handsome young artist.

"Now Bess, . . ." Nancy said soothingly.

"No, I didn't accuse Talbot of copying," the reporter responded. "But the fact remains, his picture did remind me of another painting. You see, they both portrayed an odd combination of subjects."

"What did Lee's picture show?" asked George.

"An Egyptian bust, a gray cat, and a moon in

the background. And unless I'm very much mistaken, so did another picture that I once saw right here in the River Heights Art Museum."

The three girls were somewhat taken aback by Worden's revelation.

"Golly," George muttered, "the way you describe it, Lee's painting sounds eerie! Finding two like that would be pretty unusual!"

The newsman nodded. "That's really why I came here today . . . to make sure I didn't just dream the whole thing up."

Nancy turned to her friends. "Did either of you notice such a picture?"

When both shook their heads, Nancy said to Worden, "Bess and George have just been going through the museum. Maybe you're mistaken."

The reporter's shoulders lifted in a faint shrug. "Could be. But if I'm wrong, why did he get so upset? You know that old saying, 'where there's smoke, there's fire.' Anyhow, I'm going to stroll on through and look over the collection. I always enjoy the time I spend in here."

Nancy smiled. "I know what you mean."

After Peter Worden had taken his leave of the three girls, they walked across the marble lobby and out through the heavy bronze doors into the sunshine.

As they followed a flagstone path to the parking lot, Bess said, "Gee, I could really go for a milkshake right now. How about you two?"

Her companions smiled and George said, "Nancy, I can see this poor girl's about to faint. We'd better get her some nourishment fast!"

Each took hold of one of Bess's arms. Veering off across the museum park, they walked her quickly to a nearby ice-cream parlor, where they sank into the nearest booth, laughing and out of breath.

While they waited for their orders to be served, Nancy told her two friends about the museum break-ins.

"Wow!" exclaimed Bess. "Did they take anything, Nancy?"

"Apparently not. But I have a feeling they may be back. Which reminds me, I have a phone call to make. Hold down the fort a sec."

There was a phone booth in the back of the store. Slipping in a coin, Nancy dialed Emily Owsler's number. Fortunately the retired maid was home, and she remembered how angry Louise Duval had been when the painting donated by her family was taken off the museum wall.

"Could Miss Duval's research project have had anything to do with that painting?" Nancy asked.

Emily Owsler was silent a moment before

replying. "Well, not that I know of. I remember she called in some famous art expert from New York about the painting. She wanted to get back at the museum curator and prove the painting was more valuable than he realized. But this foreign research thing was different. She was very secretive about that."

With a sigh, the maid ended, "It's too bad, dear, that I can't remember more about it. I wish I could help you."

"You already have, Miss Owsler," Nancy said gratefully. On a sudden inspiration, she added, "And maybe you can help me a bit more. Could you tell me what other interests Miss Duval had?"

"Of course. She was just crazy about playing bridge. She belonged to a club that was made up of the best women bridge-players in and around River Heights."

"Oh, great. I don't suppose you'd know if any of them are still alive?"

"As a matter of fact I do, Nancy. You see, they used to take turns playing in each other's homes, so I got to see them all quite frequently, and I remember one who was quite a bit younger than the others. Mrs. Leon Ferbury, her name was."

"And you think she may still be alive?" Nancy asked eagerly.

"Oh, I know she is," Emily Owsler declared. "I saw her picture in the paper just recently. She was giving a charity ball."

Nancy thanked the former maid and hung up with a feeling of fresh hope. Then she went back to the booth to enjoy her chocolate milkshake with Bess and George.

After driving her friends home, Nancy turned westward across town in the direction of Pierre Michaud's workshop. She felt it was time to report her progress on the case so far. She thought Pierre would be especially interested in hearing about Lisa Thorpe, and to learn that the attractive girl was still willing to help him.

Nancy parked on the cement apron outside the two-story brick building and went in. Nyra Betz, wearing a green pantsuit, looked up from her desk with a scornful sniff.

"Oh, back so soon?"

Ignoring the girl's catty tone, Nancy merely smiled and nodded. But suddenly Nyra seemed to lose her unfriendly attitude. Her glowering face took on a sly, amused look as if she were enjoying some secret joke.

Nancy was puzzled by her change in expression. Before she could take time to fathom what might be going on in Nyra's head, however, Pierre came striding out of the back room. He had on a shop apron to protect his shirt and

61

slacks, and was carrying a toolbox in one hand.

"Ah, *bonjour,* Nancy!" he exclaimed eagerly on seeing the titian-haired young sleuth. "What good news do you bring us?"

"Nothing very dramatic," she chuckled. "Just thought I'd bring you up to date on what's happened so far."

"Excellent! It is almost noon, so why not tell me over lunch?"

Nancy hesitated, slightly embarrassed that she had dropped in without thinking of the time. "Actually, I just had a milkshake. . ."

"No matter," Pierre cut in with a smile before she could refuse. "If the food does not tempt you, simply talk and I shall listen. Just give me a few moments to finish what I was doing."

The Frenchman explained that he was assembling a desktop computer model containing his new memory device. Nancy watched him install its cover, then insert and tighten the screws to hold it in place. She could not help admiring his deft, precise workmanship with tools.

"Tout fini!" he announced presently, then excused himself to go and wash up. When he returned, he had shed his apron and put on a tie and sports jacket. "Shall we go?"

Nancy felt Nyra's eyes burning a hole in her back as they went out of the workshop.

Pierre gallantly held the driver's-side door open while Nancy slid in behind the wheel, then went around the car to get in himself.

Nancy had just started the engine and was shifting into drive when Pierre exclaimed angrily, "Stop! Let me get out!"

7

The Secret Seal

Pierre flung open the car door, jumped out, and slammed it behind him. Then he strode off into his workshop.

Nancy was mystified by the young Frenchman's sudden rudeness. Up until this moment, he had always behaved with the utmost gallantry and politeness. Something must have upset him, she realized. I suppose I'd better find out what's wrong.

With a sigh, she switched off the ignition, got out, and followed him into the workshop. Pierre was standing with his back to the door, running his hands through a tray of electronic parts. From the way he would pick one up and toss it down again, he looked as though he was trying to get his temper under control.

Nyra Betz was still seated at the typewriter, tapping the keys as if unaware that anything unusual had happened. But from her smug, sidelong glance as Nancy entered the workshop and her poisonous, purse-lipped little smile, it was clear that she was thoroughly enjoying the situation.

"Do you mind telling me what's wrong, Pierre?" Nancy inquired mildly.

He swung around to face her, still flushed and fuming. "Are you implying you don't know?"

"I'm afraid I haven't the vaguest idea."

"*Très bien*, I shall show you!"

He strode out the door again, toward Nancy's trim, blue sports car. She followed him outside. Pulling open the passenger door, he pointed accusingly toward the instrument panel. "Perhaps you would care to explain *this*, Miss Drew!"

At first Nancy could not imagine what he was talking about. But when she went around to the other side of the car and slid in behind the wheel, she saw that his finger was jabbing at a small, blue-and-white sticker. It bore the name *DATA-LINC*, written in stylized script as if it were a trademark.

"Where on earth did that come from?" Nancy

murmured in surprise. When she scratched it with her fingernail, she saw that it was held in place by transparent tape.

"Are you trying to make me believe you know nothing about it?" Pierre demanded suspiciously.

"I'm not trying to make you believe anything. I never even noticed it until you pointed it out."

"Then how did that Data-Linc seal get there?"

"Hm, good question." By now, Nancy had peeled off the tape and was examining the small piece of paper bearing the blue-and-white name or emblem. "Looks as though it might have been cut off an envelope or letterhead."

Suddenly she gasped and shot a startled glance at the young Frenchman. "Wait a minute! I've just remembered something!"

"Indeed? And what is that, may I ask?"

Nancy related how her two friends had seen an unknown girl poking into her car that morning. "I assumed she was probably trying to steal something, but couldn't because my glove compartment was locked. Now it's obvious she must have been sticking this on the dashboard."

"But why? Can you answer me that?"

"Not yet," Nancy said coolly, "but I might be

66

able to make a guess if you'd tell me first why the sight of this made you so angry."

"I will certainly tell you," Pierre replied. "Data-Linc is the name of a computer company which had tried again and again to snoop on my work and harass me in every way possible. They know that as soon as my memory device comes on the market, it will make their own products out of date. So naturally they wish to stop me at any cost."

Nancy nodded thoughtfully. "I see."

"If you are working for that contemptible company," he went on in a sharp voice, "I would prefer that you drop my case at once!"

It was clear that he suspected Nancy of industrial espionage. No doubt her investigation of the Duval mystery seemed to Pierre like a perfect cover for snooping on his computer work.

The young sleuth smiled. "Don't worry, I've never even heard of the Data-Linc Company before."

Pierre's angry expression gave way to a puzzled frown. Nancy sensed that he wanted very much to believe her but was still afraid that he might be fooled. "And how do you explain the girl sticking that Data-Linc emblem inside your car?" he queried.

"Someone wanted to get me in trouble,"

Nancy replied with a shrug, "by making it look as though I had some connection with Data-Linc. Whoever did it hoped to make you so suspicious that you'd tell me to stop investigating the Duval mystery. And the plan nearly worked."

Privately, she was thinking that the mischief maker had to be someone close enough to Pierre to know about his trouble with the Data-Linc Company. Nancy reflected that this made Nyra Betz a prime suspect, especially since she seemed so jealous and resentful of Nancy's close investigating relationship with the handsome Frenchman.

In fact, the more Nancy thought about it, the better Nyra seemed to fit the role. She could have cut the emblem off an envelope or advertisement and carried it around in her purse, along with a roll of tape, just waiting for the right opportunity. And on seeing Nancy's car parked on the street that morning, she could have seized her chance.

Bess's description of the culprit as "a tall, skinny girl with sort of light brown hair" certainly fitted Nyra Betz to a T!

Meanwhile, Pierre's frown was slowly changing, first to bewilderment, then to a sheepish grin. "I fear that I have made a very foolish and hasty mistake," he said with a contrite bow.

"Can you possibly forgive me, Miss Drew?"

Nancy's blue eyes twinkled. "Okay, you're forgiven ... that is, if you promise to go on being suspicious of anything out of the ordinary, at least until we get to the bottom of this mystery. Now, how about finding a restaurant? I'm famished!"

Pierre smiled back. "I insist that you be my guest!"

As they drove away, Nancy glimpsed Nyra Betz watching them from one of the workshop windows. She looked furious.

Over a delicious lunch of chicken and avocado salad, the young sleuth filled Pierre in on the events since she had taken over the case. As Nancy expected, he was especially interested in hearing about Lisa Thorpe and pleased by the news that she still wanted to help him.

Pierre in turn related that his financial backer, Mr. Varney, was coming to the workshop tomorrow. He invited Nancy to meet him.

"Thanks, I'd like to very much," she replied. "Is he from New York City?"

"He may be. I am not sure. That is where he first got in touch with me, but now that you mention it, I am not sure where his office is located. As I may have mentioned, he seems a very modest, retiring sort of person."

Pierre explained that Varney's main interest

69

in life appeared to be helping struggling young scientists and inventors turn their ideas into successful businesses. As long as his investment of money paid off, he seemed content to remain in the background.

After driving Pierre back to his workshop, Nancy found a public telephone. Leafing through the directory, she looked up the name of the woman whom the maid, Emily Owsler, had said was a member of Louise Duval's bridge club.

Mrs. Leon Ferbury herself answered Nancy's ring. She sounded delighted at the young sleuth's phone call. "Why, of course, Miss Drew," she gushed. "I'll be glad to tell you anything I can about my dear friend Louise. How soon shall I expect you?"

"In about the ten minutes it'll take me to drive to your house," Nancy responded with a smile, "if that's convenient."

"Splendid!"

Mrs. Ferbury turned out to be a stout, bright-eyed woman with a lively manner and hair so golden that Nancy suspected its color could only have come out of a bottle. But her manner was warm and sincere.

"How exciting to be interviewed by such a famous young detective! Do sit down, dear, while I ring for tea. And I'm sure you'd like a few little cakes to nibble on."

Nancy smiled and shook her head. "Thanks, but I just finished lunch not long before I called."

"All the better! You'll love these, they're delicious little *petits fours*!"

Nancy explained that she was looking into a mysterious research project which Louise Duval had embarked on shortly before her death.

"Oh yes, I know exactly what you mean," said Mrs. Ferbury. "Poor Louise was constantly dropping hints about it."

"Then you know what the project concerned?" Nancy inquired eagerly.

"Ah, no, I'm afraid not. One could see that Louise was practically bursting to tell our bridge club all about it. But she was determined to keep her secret until all the details were worked out. Once her research man completed the project, however—oh my! Then I feel sure Louise would have made it a very exciting occasion when she announced the results!"

"I don't suppose you happen to know who the man was?"

"Oh, but of course I do, my dear! He was a

professor at Westmoor University. Let me see now ... what was his name?" Mrs. Ferbury frowned and fingered her fluffy golden hair, then showed her teeth in a sudden smile. "Oh, yes, yes, of course—I knew it would come back to me! Professor Crawford, his name was!"

Nancy felt a thrill of excitement. "Thanks ever so much, Mrs. Ferbury. You've been a tremendous help!"

Before following up this new clue, Nancy Drew had another important matter to attend to. An idea had gradually been taking shape in her mind about how to catch the museum intruders. But in order to have any chance of success, her scheme would have to be tried promptly.

Her blue car whizzed through the streets of River Heights and soon turned into the parking lot adjoining the museum building. Hurrying inside, she made her way to the curator's office on the second floor.

As she walked in, Mr. Gregory rose to his feet and beamed at the young detective. "You certainly have an uncanny sense of timing, Nancy!" he announced.

"I didn't hear any alarm go off when I walked in the lobby," she chuckled. "What is it this time?"

"My staff has just discovered what those mysterious intruders were after."

Nancy was startled. "Congratulations!" she said. "It was some valuable item in the museum's collection, I presume?"

The curator shrugged. "Well, yes and no. They were after a painting, though I'm not sure how valuable it is. To be precise, it's the painting that was presented by the Duval family when the museum first opened."

8

A Dangerous Plan

Nancy caught her breath in surprise. The Duval family again! This *had* to be more than a coincidence, she felt.

"How did you staff find out the intruders were trying to steal that particular painting?" she asked the curator.

"Because it's gone."

Nancy was dismayed at this unexpected news. Now more than ever she was convinced that the stolen painting must be connected in some way with the mystery of Louise Duval's letter to Pierre's grandfather. But with the picture gone, she might never learn what linked the two cases.

"Exactly how was the robbery discovered?" she asked, probing for a clue.

Mr. Gregory explained that when the stack of

crates was knocked over in the basement storage area during the second break-in, several were smashed open and their contents spilled out.

"It was rather a mess," he went on, "especially since the whole storage area is littered and long overdue for a cleanup. Anyhow, to make sure everything was restored to its proper place, my staff had to check and make sure each item got put back where it belonged."

"How did they do that?"

"When anything is assigned to storage," Mr. Gregory replied, "it's logged by its number in the museum collection. Its storage location is also entered in the logbook, and by that I mean the crate or rack or shelf on which the object will be placed. I'd already asked the staffers to bring up the Duval painting for you to look at, so while they were going through the logbook, they decided to attend to that at the same time. But when they went to get the painting, they found out it was missing from its slot in the rack."

Nancy knit her brow thoughtfully. "If that's the case, the robbers may have taken other things too," she said, "but perhaps your staff just hasn't discovered they're missing yet."

The balding curator nodded. "That's possible, of course. But, you see, something else happened which also indicates the thieves were after the Duval painting."

"What was that?" Nancy inquired with keen interest.

"One of my staff assistants, Miss Heron, now tells me she had a phone call about it on the afternoon before the second break-in."

Mr. Gregory related that the caller had asked where the Duval painting was hung, saying he had looked for it during a recent visit to the museum but hadn't been able to find it. Miss Heron then informed him that the picture was no longer on display, that it had been taken down to the basement storage area some years ago.

"This could have been what led the intruders to search the storage room," the curator surmised.

Nancy was inclined to agree. "Actually, I came to offer a suggestion. But from what you've just told me, I guess it's too late to do any good," she added with a rueful smile.

"What did you have in mind, Nancy?"

Before the pretty young sleuth could reply, there was a knock on the door.

"Excuse me a moment," Mr. Gregory said to her, then called out, "Come in!"

An attractive young woman with curly dark hair opened the door. She was wearing a rather rumpled, soiled-looking smock with the sleeves pushed up to her elbows. On seeing Nancy, she apologized for interrupting, and Mr. Gregory introduced her as the staff assistant he had mentioned earlier, Jane Heron.

"I'm afraid we misinformed you about the Duval painting," she told the curator.

His eyebrows lifted in surprise. "You've found it?"

"No, but this afternoon we've discovered that other paintings and art objects are also missing from their proper places. And some have turned up in the *wrong* places."

Mr. Gregory frowned in annoyance. "That sounds as though the whole storage area's in a state of mixup."

"I'm afraid so," Miss Heron agreed. "Whoever broke in the other night may be partly responsible, but I'd say everything down there's gotten pretty disordered over the years. So we won't really know if the Duval painting is missing until everything's been sorted out."

Under the circumstances, Nancy decided to tell the curator the idea which she had come to suggest in the first place. Before doing so, however, she waited until Miss Heron left the office. Then she asked if he had considered the possibility that the break-ins might be an inside job, with someone at the museum helping the intruders.

Mr. Gregory nodded gloomily. "Yes, there's

always that chance, I'm afraid. Why do you ask?"

"Suppose you let on, both to the staff and to the public, that the repairmen have run into trouble, and the alarm system isn't fixed yet."

"You mean as bait, to tempt the thieves into trying again?"

"Exactly! And I'll keep watch in the museum tonight myself," Nancy went on, "to see if they do come back."

The curator looked worried. "Nancy, what you're suggesting could be dangerous—very dangerous!"

"Not really, Mr. Gregory. I'll bring a friend or two along to keep me company, and if an emergency should arise, we'll call for help at once. We can keep in touch with the night watchman by walkie-talkie, and also stay close to a phone so we can ring the police if necessary."

Somewhat reluctantly, the curator agreed to her plan. He said the repairmen expected to have the alarm system back in working order by mid-afternoon, but he would arrange privately to have them stay on till the end of the day. He would also tell them to leave their ladders and other working paraphernalia in place, and go off grumbling and shaking their heads, so as to give the impression that they had encountered unforeseen difficulties that kept them from finishing the job and hooking up the alarm again.

Nancy said good-bye to Mr. Gregory and went back down to the lobby, hopeful that her plan would produce prompt results.

Coming out of the museum, she glimpsed a figure standing in the bus shelter, just beyond the green parklike stretch of lawn. He seemed to be watching the museum entrance. The man looked familiar.

Nancy paused to stare more carefully, then gasped. It's that swarthy thug again! she realized. The one who keeps spying on me!

This time Nancy decided not to let him get away. She started boldly down the front walk of the museum, heading toward the bus shelter. But the dark-visaged spy saw her coming. With a scowl, he darted off across the street.

Before Nancy could reach the corner and cross, the traffic light turned red against her. Vehicles rumbled across the intersection, blocking her path of pursuit. By now, the swarthy man was fast disappearing from view among the passersby on the other side.

Nancy realized she had no chance of catching him now. With a sigh of annoyance, she gave up and turned back toward the museum parking lot.

Driving home, Nancy looked forward to a hot

cup of Hannah's skillfully brewed tea. To her surprise and delight, she found Bess Marvin and George Fayne waiting for her in the living room.

"Any exciting developments?" George asked with a twinkle.

"How would you like to help me catch some crooks?" Nancy proposed.

Her words brought both girls instantly to attention.

"Gee, Nancy! What do you want us to do?" asked Bess, opening her blue eyes wide.

"Tell you in a minute. First, though, do you remember that girl you saw poking into my car this morning?"

Bess nodded. "Sure we do. What about her?"

"Can you recall what she was wearing?"

After a moment's thought, Bess and George agreed that she had been wearing a green pantsuit. This confirmed Nancy's hunch that the culprit was probably Nyra Betz.

Then the young detective described her plan to stake out the art museum that night. She asked if her friends would like to help her keep watch for possible intruders. Bess and George eagerly agreed.

The three girls enjoyed a relaxing afternoon tea. Later, they all piled into Nancy's car. She dropped the two cousins off at their homes to get ready for their night watch session. Then she drove to nearby Westmoor U. to follow up the lead Mrs. Ferbury had given her.

Nancy was already acquainted with some of the faculty members at Westmoor. On this occasion, however, an unexpected obstacle was in store. The dean of students informed her that Professor Crawford, a history instructor, had passed away several years ago.

Nancy's face showed her disappointment. "Oh, dear! Is there anyone else who might be able to answer some questions about his work?"

"Hm, well, I suppose the best person to ask might be Professor Schmidt. He's the person who took over Professor Crawford's position in the history department."

Professor Schmidt turned out to be a friendly, pipe-smoking, middle-aged man. But when Nancy asked him if he had any idea what sort of research work Professor Crawford might have done for the late Miss Duval, he shook his head.

"I'm sorry, but I really have no idea." He added after a moment's thought, "One would imagine, of course, that it would have concerned his particular specialty."

"What was that?" Nancy inquired.

"He specialized in the history of the French Revolution and the Napoleonic Wars."

Nancy felt a surge of hope. "Roughly, that would be around 1800?"

Professor Schmidt nodded. "Yes, both before and after that date. Say from the 1780s to 1815."

This was about the time that Louise Duval's ancestress, Yvette Duval, had immigrated to America and settled in River Heights!

Professor Schmidt frowned as he paused to reload his pipe. "Perhaps if you spoke to Professor Crawford's daughter," he went on, "she might be able to supply the information you need."

"Do you know how I could get in touch with her?" asked Nancy, crossing her fingers.

"Yes, she lives not too far from here. I think I have her address in my desk book."

Nancy drove home, feeling much encouraged. Over the dinner table, she told her father and Hannah Gruen about the day's events.

"Why not ask the town historical society about that French couple?" the housekeeper suggested. "They have all sorts of information about the early settlers in River Heights."

Nancy beamed. "Hannah, that's a wonderful idea! I never even thought of that."

After dinner, she picked up her two friends

and drove to the art museum. However, instead of parking in the museum lot Nancy left her car a block away, and they approached the building on foot. It was already twilight, but to make doubly sure no one observed them, the trio went to the back door of the museum in the gathering darkness.

The night watchman answered their knock and opened the heavy metal door. "'Evening, girls. Sure you want to go through with this scheme?"

Nancy smiled. "Quite sure, Mr. Baxter. If we can keep in touch with you, I think we'll be okay."

Shaking his head dubiously, the watchman took them down to the basement storage area. Before leaving them alone, he provided them with a walkie-talkie which they could use to call him.

The vast, cement-walled room was carefully air-conditioned. Just now, it was strewn with crates, as well as wrappings that had been removed by the staff in order to check out individual paintings and other stored art objects.

For a while, the items were interesting to look over. But as time passed, the girls settled down to chat and sip coffee from Thermoses they had brought to help keep awake.

Suddenly George sat upright and raised her hand for silence. "What was that?" she whispered.

Clank . . . clank . . . clank.

Faint, metallic footsteps could be heard coming down the hallway!

9

Spook in Armor

Wide-eyed, the girls looked at each other in alarm. Shakily, Bess whispered, "Oh, Nancy, quick, call Mr. Baxter!"

George, white-faced and nervous with her eyes glued to the door to the corridor, chimed in, "That's a good idea!"

Nancy switched on the walkie-talkie and spoke to the night watchman. "Mr. Baxter, this is Nancy Drew. Come quickly, please!"

There was no response.

The clanking footsteps had stopped and the doorknob was slowly turning as she called more urgently, "Mr. Baxter! Someone's coming into the storage room! Answer please!"

Again there was no reply from the walkie-talkie.

Transfixed with fright, the three girls

watched as the door swung open. They could hardly believe what they saw next.

The metal-shod intruder who clanked slowly into the room was a ghostly figure in armor!

Earlier in the evening, after looking over the paintings and uncrated art objects, the girls had shut off all except one of the bright fluorescent ceiling lights. The shadowy gloom added to the spooky appearance of their strange visitor.

"Oh, no!" Bess gulped in a squeaky whisper. "We must be seeing things!"

In one gauntleted fist, the spectral knight was clutching a halberd, a spearlike weapon with a broad ax close to its pointed tip. The figure's visor was down, preventing them from seeing any face inside the helmet.

Bess and George backed away in terror as the armoured specter came stalking toward them. Suddenly it swung the long weapon, knocking the walkie-talkie out of Nancy's hand with the flat side of the ax blade!

Her own knees weak with fright, Nancy yielded to panic and followed her two friends. The girls retreated into a small side room used for record-keeping and filing. But they were still not safe, as they quickly discovered when they tried to lock the door.

"There's n-n-no key!" George hissed, fumbling frantically in the dark.

In desperation, all three girls leaned against the door, waiting to hold it shut should the weird intruder try to come after them.

Minutes passed and . . . nothing happened!

By this time, Nancy had regained her calm. Bravely she decided to open the door and confront the armored spook.

"No, Nancy!" Bess begged. "Don't go out there! Let's just wait in here. Maybe it'll go away!"

"Don't worry, I'll be careful," Nancy promised. Putting her fingers to her lips, she slowly opened the door and peeked out.

The figure in armor was just turning away with a faint chuckle, evidently satisfied that he had frightened the three girls enough to keep them from giving him any trouble. He had laid down his halberd on a crate just behind him, and now was about to look through some of the paintings.

If only she could reach the halberd without being heard!

Taking a deep breath, Nancy tiptoed back into the main storage room. Step by step, she crept stealthily toward the weapon.

Just as she reached out and put her hand on the halberd, the ghostly knight turned! He had pushed up the visor of his helmet, and a pair of eyes glittered fiendishly out at her!

Swiftly Nancy snatched up the weapon and swung it. The flat of the ax smacked against the knight's helmet, staggering him!

He lurched toward the door, apparently dazed. Nancy darted in pursuit and whacked him again, this time almost knocking him down. But he managed to plunge out the door and slam it shut behind him!

Nancy uttered a faint groan of dismay as she tried the knob again and again but could not turn it. By this time, George and Bess had ventured out of their hiding place and were hurrying to join her.

"We're locked in!" she told them.

"Oh golly, Nancy, you were so brave! I was too petrified to do anything!" Bess said.

"Same here," George admitted a bit sheepishly. Putting her hands on her hips, she gazed all around, looking for another exit through which they might reach the stairway leading up to the main floor. "What do we do now, sit and wait?"

Nancy shook her head vigorously. "No, I'm going to get this door opened!"

"How?" asked Bess, none too hopefully.

"Just let me get my purse, and maybe I can show you."

Her friends followed Nancy across the room to where they had left their purses on one of the worktables. Then the other two watched as she began rummaging through her bag.

"What are you looking for, Nancy?" asked George.

"Oh, gosh ... a bobbypin, a hairpin, a nail file," Nancy said as she emptied out the contents of her brown leather shoulder bag. "Something I can use to pick that door lock."

Bess and George now followed suit and began to search their own bags.

"I might just have a bobby pin in here somewhere," Bess said. "It's been so long since I emptied this out. . . ." Her voice trailed off.

"Eureka! This may do it," Nancy exclaimed, holding up a paper clip.

Going back to the door, she unbent the clip and inserted one end in the lock. Then she began to probe delicately, moving the wire this way and that.

After many breathless moments, the three heard a click!

Nancy removed the paper clip, then turned to Bess and George, putting one finger to her lips. "I doubt if that spook is still out there, but let's not take any chances."

Very quietly, she opened the door a crack and

peered out. She could see no one in the corridor. Encouraged, she cautiously pushed the door open the rest of the way.

Their unpleasant visitor was gone.

"Thank heavens!" George breathed in relief.

The only trace left of the phantom knight was a carelessly discarded pile of armor.

Nancy telephoned the police. Then, confident that the intruder or intruders had fled, the girls began a hasty search for the missing watchman. They found him on the second floor as they passed the open doorway of the curator's office.

"There he is!" Bess gasped fearfully.

Mr. Baxter lay sprawled on the floor near the curator's desk. There were two telephones on the desk. The receiver of one was hanging over the edge, dangling at the end of its cord.

The girls hurried to attend to the unconscious watchman. George knelt beside the elderly man and felt his pulse.

"Is he all right?" her cousin asked, holding one hand pressed anxiously to her cheek as she watched.

George nodded. "I think so. Smells as if he's been chloroformed or given ether."

Nancy hurried off to the water fountain in the corridor and moistened her handkerchief. Just as she returned to the office, Mr. Baxter began to groan. George raised his head and shoulders slightly while Nancy bathed his forehead with the cool, damp cloth.

Presently the watchman's eyes flickered open and he struggled to sit up. Once he had gotten his bearings, he told the girls that while he was patroling inside the building, he had heard the phone ringing in the curator's office.

"I went in to answer it, and just as I picked up the receiver, someone grabbed me in a bear hug from behind. Then another guy held a cloth over my nose and mouth. That's that last I remember until now."

At the girls' insistence, the elderly man sat resting in an armchair until the police arrived.

A cruiser was first on the scene, followed soon afterward by a squad car from police headquarters. Two detectives listened carefully to the girls' story and promised that the armor would be dusted for fingerprints. Then a uniformed officer escorted them to Nancy's parked car. The young policeman even wanted to have the cruiser shepherd them safely home, but Nancy laughingly declined.

Next morning over a breakfast of sausages and pancakes, Nancy told her father and Hannah about the night's events at the museum.

Carson Drew looked thoughtful and re-marked, "I believe I'll drop in on Police Chief McGinnis today and see what they've found out."

The housekeeper's kindly face had taken on a worried expression. "Nancy, this case sounds as though it's getting dangerous," she said.

The sleuth grinned across the table. "Not really. It's just getting exciting."

A few moments later she finished her coffee, got up from her chair, and kissed her father good-bye. "I'm going to follow your suggestion, Hannah," Nancy announced, "and pay a visit to the River Heights Historical Society."

Soon afterward, she was pulling up her car in front of its destination. The historical society was housed appropriately in an old Victorian mansion bequeathed to it by a long-dead member.

Inside, Nancy was greeted by the friendly, white-haired secretary of the society, Mr. George Teakin. He listened to her request and seemed delighted at a chance to help the famous young detective.

"Let me just make a note of what you're after," he said, pulling a small, leather-bound notebook out of his coat pocket. After jotting down the details, he added, "This may take a while, Miss Drew, but I'll check through all the old newspapers of that period and see if I can find any news items about the Duvals."

"I'd really appreciate it, Mr. Teakin. Thank you ever so much."

Slipping behind the wheel of her sports car again, Nancy headed back to the River Heights Art Museum. As she drove through the busy morning streets, she reviewed last night's happenings in her mind.

If only I'd been able to catch that crook in armor, she thought, I'd have the answer to one mystery right now!

Arriving at the museum, Nancy inquired for Mr. Gregory and was told that he was down in the basement storage area. In a few moments she was opening the door of the big, brightly lit, cement-walled room.

The curator was nowhere in sight, but a dark-haired young woman in a smock was sorting out a group of paintings. Nancy recognized her as his assistant, Jane Heron.

"Is Mr. Gregory around?" Nancy asked, walking toward her.

Miss Heron looked up and greeted her with a smile. "He was here just a minute ago," she replied. "He must have stepped out somewhere."

Nancy caught her breath as she suddenly

noticed a painting which the curator's assistant had just laid aside.

It showed a sphinxlike statuette and a gray cat in a desert landscape, with the moon rising eerily behind them!

10

Damaging Evidence

Nancy was astonished. She knew at once that this must be the painting which the reporter, Peter Worden, had described to her and her friends.

No wonder he had spoken out so frankly and refused to back down, despite the artist's angry indignation!

The picture was small and seemed to Nancy not very impressive in style and artistry. It might not have even looked much like the painting that had won Lee Talbot first prize at the Riverview Art Show. But if Worden was telling the truth, the choice of those same three subjects—an Egyptian bust and a gray cat, with the moon in the background—was at the very least an odd coincidence.

But what should she do about it? Nancy was troubled. She had no wish to become involved in an ugly name-calling dispute. On the other hand, if Lee Talbot had deliberately copied another artist's work, it seemed unfair that he should win first prize at such an important art show.

With a sigh, Nancy decided to ponder the matter for a while and perhaps ask her father's advice before taking any steps. Meanwhile, it might be well to snap a photo of the museum painting to compare with the other later on, in case he did advise her to notify the art show judges.

Nancy turned to Miss Heron and pointed to the eerie-looking canvas. "Mind if I set this up in brighter light somewhere, so I can photograph it?"

"Of course not. Go right ahead." The curator's assistant looked slightly surprised at the teenager's request, but politely refrained from asking the reason.

Nancy laid the painting on a worktable directly under one of the fluorescent ceiling lights and proceeded to snap a picture of it with her tiny purse camera.

She had just finished when Mr. Gregory came into the room. "Oh, there you are,

Nancy," he exclaimed on seeing her. "I heard you were here. That was quite an adventure you had last night."

"The intruder certainly turned up in an unusual disguise," she chuckled.

"So I gather. And I think I can show you just how it happened."

The balding curator led Nancy to a small basement workshop down the hall and showed her scratch marks on the door lock, indicating that it had been jimmied open.

"Rather a clumsy job," she observed thoughtfully, "or else a hasty one."

Mr. Gregory nodded. "The latter, I think. They probably sneaked down here just before closing time and had to find a place to hide quickly before anyone noticed them."

He added that regular museum craftsmen employed in the workshop had found cigarette butts and an empty matchbook in the room when they came to work that morning.

Looking around inside the workshop, Nancy saw various pieces of armor being repaired.

"So this is where one of them got the idea of dressing up like a spooky knight to scare us!"

"Exactly," the curator agreed. "What I still don't understand is just how they contrived to ambush the watchman."

"I think I can explain that," the young detective said. "especially now that you've shown me how they entered in the first place."

Nancy conjectured that after the museum had closed and the staff had gone home, one of the thieves had emerged from the basement workshop, made his way cautiously upstairs, and picked the lock on the curator's office door.

"You have a special private telephone in your office, don't you?" Nancy paused to inquire. "I mean, besides the regular museum phone line."

"Yes, in the telephone directory, under River Heights Art Museum, you'll find it listed separately as 'Curator's Office' with its own separate number."

Nancy suggested that while one intruder stationed himself in the curator's office, another could have furtively spied on the watchman as he patroled the museum.

"Then when he saw the watchman go upstairs, he could have dialed your office number from one of the pay phones on the main floor."

"Ah, I see what you mean!" said Mr. Gregory. "That's how the watchman just 'happened' to hear the phone ringing as he went past my office."

"Right," Nancy declared. "Then when he went in to answer it, the one lying in wait pounced on him. And the one who'd done the dialing hurried upstairs to help subdue their victim."

"I believe you've hit on the explanation, Nancy. And incidentally, I would say this pretty well eliminates the theory that they may have had an inside helper."

Nancy agreed with the curator. "If a museum employee had fallen into our trap and tipped them off that the alarm system was still disconnected, they wouldn't have bothered hiding out in that basement workshop."

Mr. Gregory thanked the young detective for her help and promised to notify her at once if the Duval family painting turned up in the storage area.

Nancy then left the museum and drove to the newspaper office of the River Heights *Record*. At the reception desk in the lobby, she asked to speak to the arts and entertainment reporter, Peter Worden, and was promptly directed upstairs to his cubbyhole office.

Worden greeted her with a smile. "How can I help you, Nancy?"

"Could you give me a more detailed description of Lee Talbot's prize-winning painting?" she asked, returning his smile.

"I can do better than that. I can show you a photograph of it."

Leafing through a file drawer, Peter Worden pulled out a glossy 8 × 10 photograph. It showed Talbot and the art show judges grouped around his painting, which looked quite large.

Nancy was startled, but not by the size of the canvas. Pictorially speaking, Lee Talbot's work was an almost precise duplicate of the smaller painting that she had seen just a short time before!

The newsman noticed her gasp of surprise. "Is there anything you care to tell me, Nancy?" he asked discreetly.

Nancy Drew hesitated. Since Peter Worden was the one who had first apprised her of the suspicious similarity, and had now helped her prove it beyond a doubt, she felt she at least owed him a word of explanation.

"I can only speak off the record," she said unhappily. "If I do, will you promise not to quote me, or involve me in any way in your dispute with Lee Talbot?"

"Of course I'll promise. You have my word of honor on that, Nancy."

"Then I'm sorry to say your suspicions were right. The painting you remembered happens to be down in the basement storage area of the museum." She told him the size of the picture and the name of the artist who had painted it.

The whole episode left Nancy feeling rather

heavyhearted and depressed. Nevertheless, she dropped off her film at a camera store to be developed. Then she headed out of town.

Maybe a drive in the country will cheer me up, she told herself hopefully.

Professor Crawford's married daughter lived in a pleasant rural hamlet about a dozen miles from River Heights. Her name was Mrs. Grale and she herself was now a parent with two children of school age.

She received Nancy in a friendly way, and they sat down to chat in her kitchen over cups of instant coffee. But she shook her head regretfully to Nancy's question.

"Remember, I was only a little girl at the time you speak of. I imagine in those days I hardly even realized my dad was a history prof," Mrs. Grale added with a smile.

"Then you've no idea what kind of research he may have carried out for Miss Louise Duval?"

"I'm afraid not, dear. You see, I turned over all his academic papers and records to Westmoor U. after he died."

Nancy thanked Mrs. Grale and rose to leave.

"I'm sorry I can't be of any more help, Miss Drew, after you've come all this way," the woman said as they stood in the doorway.

Nancy smiled cheerfully. "That's all right. I really enjoyed the ride."

On her way back to River Heights, Nancy stopped off at a delightful old inn for a late lunch. Then, with an eye on the time, she sped back to town to keep her appointment at Pierre's workshop, where she was to meet his backer, Mr. Varney.

Nancy felt somewhat out of place when she found the young Frenchman talking to a shrewd-looking, businesslike individual named Marston Parker. Aparently they had been discussing the technical details of Pierre's computer memory device.

"Don't let me interrupt," Nancy said hastily. "Why don't I come back a bit later when you're free, Picrre?"

"No, no! Please stay," he insisted. "Mr. Parker represents one of your big American computer companies, and I am about to demonstrate my invention to him. This is a chance for you to see what my work is all about, Nancy, and perhaps if my demonstration is successful, it will also mark the first step in an important business deal."

Nancy's blue eyes twinkled. "Very well. If you don't mind an audience, I'll sit and watch."

Pierre bustled about, preparing the demonstration. This would involve the desktop computer model that she had seen him assembling the day before. He looked annoyed at the fact that some of his tools seemed to be out of place, and as a result he could not lay hands promptly on a particular one that he needed.

"My assistant, Nyra Betz, is home ill today," he explained, "and I cannot seem to find anything when I need it. She must have moved things around before we closed up the shop yesterday evening."

At last, however, all was ready. Pierre was speaking to Mr. Parker, just before flicking a switch that would turn on the computer.

Nancy felt vaguely uneasy for some reason that she could not understand. Then she noticed several scratch marks around the screws holding the cover of the computer in place. Perhaps the scratches on the door lock of the museum workshop had made her especially aware of such evidence.

"Those scratches weren't there yesterday," she murmured with a frown.

They were also completely out of character with Pierre's deft, craftsmanlike way with tools. He would never have driven in screws so carelessly as to mar the glossy finish of the plastic cover.

A sudden, dismaying thought flashed through

Nancy's mind. The young Frenchman was about to press the switch that would turn on power to the computer.

"Pierre, don't!" she cried out in alarm.

But it was too late to stop him. An instant later, a loud explosion echoed through the workshop as the computer blew up!

11

English Settlers

Warned by Nancy's cry, Pierre and Marston Parker had drawn back and flung their arms over their faces. So despite the force of the blast and the flying debris, no one was hurt except for some scratches and bruises. But the computer itself was badly damaged, as was Pierre's invention.

"What went wrong?" Parker asked, frowning and obviously disturbed by what had happened.

"I'm afraid the setup was booby-trapped," put in Nancy, and she explained what had aroused her suspicions. "Evidently, someone doesn't want Pierre to succeed in selling his memory device."

The young Frenchman was at first bewildered, then grim and tight-lipped, as he surveyed the results of the blast. "Obviously I cannot go on with the demonstration. My equipment is ruined. I apologize for wasting your time, Mr. Parker."

"Too bad," the manufacturer's agent commiserated, although he seemed not wholly convinced by Nancy's explanation of the explosion. "Does this set you back very far?"

"I have lost about a month's work," Pierre said in a discouraged voice. "Not to mention the cost of replacing the parts that have been destroyed." Then he shrugged and smiled bravely. "*Eh bien*, thank goodness no one was hurt."

There was a sharp rap on the half-open door. A big, vigorous-looking man in his fifties entered the workshop and looked around in astonishment. "Well, well! I'd say something violent occurred here. What happened?"

"Ah, Mr. Varney!" Pierre hurried toward his visitor, hand outstretched. "You come at an unfortunate time. Some unknown enemy has sabotaged my work."

"I warned you to be on the lookout for trouble, son." Varney, who had the tanned, weathered face of an outdoor sportsman, was frowning. "Did anyone see anything suspicious?"

He flung a questioning glance at Marston Parker and Nancy.

"Miss Drew is quite famous for solving mysteries," Pierre explained. "Luckily, she detected trouble just in time to save us from injury."

After introducing his guests to each other, Pierre added to Nancy, "You remember I told you that Mr. Varney is financing my work."

"Oh yes, of course." Nancy smiled at the big man. "How lucky for Pierre that you're helping him. How did you happen to hear of him?"

"Miss Drew, all my friends know that I'm on the lookout for promising young business people and inventors. So they keep me well informed."

As Nancy nodded, he went on. "Now, in Pierre's case, a friend in Europe saw an interview with him and a report on his computer work in a French newspaper. After reading that Pierre was about to come to the U.S.A., he notified me."

Varney turned to Pierre, who had just seen Marston Parker out the door. "By the way, my boy, have a list ready this afternoon of whatever you'll need to replace all this damaged material. My secretary will call you."

Pierre thanked him sincerely.

The financier clapped the young Frenchman on the back, saying, "In the meantime, don't be too downhearted." Then he smiled at Nancy—

"A pleasure to have met you, Miss Drew"—and left.

The girl detective looked at Pierre. "You look considerably more cheerful, I'm glad to see."

"*Vraiment*." He smiled. Then his face became somewhat more serious. "Nancy, I've been meaning to ask if you have had any further word from Lisa—er, Miss Thorpe. Do you think . . ."

He paused uncertainly.

Nancy replied, "I'm glad you reminded me. I must phone her. May I call from here?"

"Oh, but of course," Pierre said eagerly.

"Would you care to speak to her when I'm through? I'm sure she'd like to hear from you," Nancy said as she dialed Lisa's number.

A servant's voice answered, but Lisa herself soon came on the line. Nancy explained that she was calling from Pierre Michaud's workshop, then asked, "Lisa, did your great-aunt, Louise Duval, leave any personal belongings or papers that are still in your family's possession?"

"Let me think." After a moment's pause, Lisa said, "I'm not certain. But there are lots of old family things, trunks and so on, in the attic. There may even be things going back to Paul and Yvette Duval's time."

"Oh, wonderful!" Nancy exclaimed. "You

see, I've been wondering if Miss Louise might have left anything among her personal effects that would shed some light on her letter to Pierre's grandfather."

"It's certainly possible." Lisa cleared her throat nervously. "Nancy, why don't you come over tomorrow afternoon and we'll go through the stuff together."

Nancy hesitated. "I'd love to, but are you sure it won't . . ."

Lisa interrupted, "Don't worry, my father won't be here. And anyway, it's my house too," she finished boldly.

Nancy laughed. "Fine. See you then. Now, here's Pierre, who'd like a word with you before I hang up." And she handed the phone to him.

Gathering up her purse and car keys, Nancy waved goodbye to the young inventor. He was already deeply engrossed in conversation and barely seemed to notice her departure as she slipped out the door with a smile.

Nancy drove home and had no sooner arrived in the house when the telephone rang. Hannah Gruen, the Drews' housekeeper, answered it.

"Just a moment, please," she said, then with her hand over the mouthpiece murmured to Nancy, "It's for you, dear. A Mr. Teakin."

Dropping her shoulder bag on a chair near the door, Nancy took the receiver from Hannah.

"Miss Drew," the pleasant voice of the historical society's secretary greeted her, "I've found something that may interest you, so I thought I'd let you know right away."

"Oh good, Mr. Teakin! What did you find?"

"A local newspaper article, dated in 1796. It tells how Paul and Yvette Duval had just settled in River Heights."

Nancy listened with keen interest as he went on. "According to this report, they arrived here from London, England, and it goes on to say that Paul Duval had been a director of the Mercantile Exchange Bank there for the past six years."

After exchanging a few more remarks with the society secretary, Nancy thanked him for the helpful information and hung up, surprised and puzzled.

Despite their French name and the family tradition of their French background, the Duval couple had come from England! In fact, from what the newspaper article told about them, they might not have been French at all. At any rate, they had apparently been living in England for some time before coming to America.

Nancy spent the rest of the afternoon mulling

over what bearing all this might have on the mystery.

Just before dinner, as Nancy was helping Hannah set the table, Lisa Thorpe called. She asked if Nancy could come to her house that evening instead of tomorrow afternoon.

"Of course, Lisa, no problem. About eight-fifteen or so? Fine. See you then."

The Drews and Hannah sat down to a leisurely dinner of lamb chops and minted peas, topped off by a flaky-crusted blueberry pie for dessert. Afterward, Carson Drew left to keep an appointment with a client, while Nancy helped Hannah clear the table and load the dishwasher.

Then, running a comb through her hair, Nancy slipped on a beige raincoat and started out for Lisa's house.

It was a cloudy, windy evening with a promise of rain in the air. As Nancy parked in front of the Thorpes' house, the first few drops of rain began to spatter the windshield.

Lisa answered the door with a welcoming smile. Taking Nancy's raincoat, she whispered, "I have an unexpected guest, I'm afraid," and then led her into a charmingly decorated drawing room.

A blond, wavy-haired young man stood up to greet the new arrival. "Ah, Miss Drew! You do get around, don't you?" he said in his affected, man-of-the world voice. To Lisa he added by way of explanation, "We met just the other day at the art museum."

Settling himself on the sofa again, Lee Talbot crossed his legs gracefully and went on, "Lisa and I were just enjoying a cozy evening for two. I'd no idea she was expecting company."

His remark seemed to imply that he and Lisa were romantically involved, and that Nancy was intruding. But from the look on Lisa's face, she could see that this was far from the truth. Nancy suspected that he felt somewhat embarrassed over her having witnessed his unpleasant scene with Peter Worden, so now he was trying to assert an air of suave superiority.

To change the subject, Nancy asked politely if he had done any more painting recently.

"Oh yes! I have two or three exciting new canvases under way." Springing up from the sofa again, Lee Talbot began to describe his new works of art with elaborate gestures. "I rather think my next exhibit wil cause quite a stir in the art world," he informed the two girls with a smirk.

Nancy found him unpleasantly smug and boring. So did Lisa, apparently. When he paused by her chair and casually slipped an arm around her shoulder, Lisa gently but firmly disengaged herself.

Undeterred by her coolness, Talbot went on in his self-satisfied way to relate how impressed the judges at the recent art show had been by his prize-winning picture.

"I've seen a photograph of it since we met," Nancy put in. "You certainly chose an exotic and unusual subject. May I ask where you got the inspiration for your painting?"

Instead of looking pleased at her question, Lee Talbot's face darkened with anger. "What's that supposed to mean?" he snapped. "I suppose you've been talking with that ignorant lout, Worden. Well, you can tell him from me he's asking for trouble and a possible lawsuit!"

With a curt apology and good-night to Lisa, he stalked out of the room. A moment later, the startled girls heard the front door slam, then a car engine rev up and zoom off.

As if to punctuate his departure, a violent thunderclap rumbled through the sky, and the storm burst in full fury!

12

A Ghost in the Attic

The outbreak of the storm seemed to relieve Lisa Thorpe's pent-up emotional tension. She gave a nervous giggle of relief. "It's awful of me to say so, Nancy, but I'm glad he's gone!"

Nancy grinned understandingly. "I was about to apologize for driving your guest away. But if you don't mind, I guess I don't either."

Lisa shook her head in mock regret. "Poor Lee. He's such a stuffed shirt and doesn't even realize it. He thinks he's the art world's gift to women."

"Actually, I got the impression he considers you two practically engaged."

"My father wishes we were," Lisa confided unhappily. "Lee's quite rich, you see, so Daddy thinks we'd be a good match. But personally I can't stand him—he's such a bore! All he ever talks about is himself and his great artistic talent."

"Does your father often try to make decisions for you?" Nancy inquired gently.

"All the time!" Lisa seemed only too eager to pour out her troubles to a sympathetic listener. "Daddy's always been like that, ever since Mother died when I was ten—I mean, bossing me around, telling me how to act, where to go, what to do and what not to do."

She went on less resentfully, as if trying to see both points of view. "He means well, I suppose. He probably tries to be both a mother and father to me. The trouble is, his idea of mothering is overseeing everything I do—nagging me to do this or that—pecking at me like a mother hen. Or a mother rooster, if you can imagine such a thing!" Lisa added with another nervous giggle. "I guess you can't really know what it's like, though, unless you've lost your own mother."

"As a matter of fact, I have," Nancy responded quietly. "My mother died when I was three. But we have a very kind-hearted, motherly housekeeper, who helped to make up for the loss. And being a lawyer, Dad tends to persuade people rather than boss them around. Your father's a business tycoon, isn't he? . . . so

I suppose he's probably more used to issuing orders and having them obeyed."

"That's Daddy, all right!" Lisa nodded vigorously.

From the other girl's timid yet outspoken manner, as if she were saying things she'd never before dared to express openly, Nancy sensed that Lisa was scared of her father and his dictatorial ways. At the same time, a bond of sympathy was already forming between the two girls because both had been motherless since an early age.

Lisa related that her mother was the daughter of Louise Duval's twin brother, Louis, who had moved abroad with his family while pursuing his career as a diplomat. Later, after his daughter grew up, she had returned to River Heights and married Norton Thorpe.

Even though the latter was rich and autocratic, it was still not clear to Nancy why he had taken such an instant dislike to Pierre Michaud.

"Since your mother lived abroad for so long," Nancy remarked, "maybe she would have been more friendly toward Pierre than your father seems to be."

Lisa nodded reflectively. "Yes, I think she might have. Somehow I feel Great-Aunt Louise

117

would have approved of him too, even though from what Mother used to tell me, she was quite regal and stuffy in her own way."

Lisa said that after Louise Duval's death, the family decided her mansion was too large and costly to keep up, so it was finally sold and torn down to make way for an industrial park.

"There must have been many old possessions of the Duval family in her mansion," Nancy said thoughtfully. "Do you know what happened to them when the house was sold?"

"I believe most of the furnishings were sold along with it. But Mother probably had the family items moved here. Anyhow, there's certainly a lot of old-fashioned junk and paraphernalia up in the attic, Nancy, and you're welcome to look through it."

The storm was still raging outside, though not as loudly as before. During a lull in the conversation, the girls suddenly heard creaky footsteps somewhere overhead.

"What was that?" Lisa exclaimed.

From her startled expression, Nancy saw that the sounds were quite unexpected.

"Footsteps, I think. Is anyone else in the house?"

"Just Booker. He's Daddy's old valet and man-servant. But he's out in the kitchen, I'm sure! And those footsteps sounded high up—almost as if they were coming from the attic!"

Lisa's timid nature was apparent from her look of growing alarm. Putting the situation into words seemed to frighten her even more—especially after she went to check on Booker and found him shining silverware in the pantry.

Just as Lisa returned to the drawing room, followed by the elderly servant, several more faint creaks were heard from above.

"I think we should call the police, Nancy, don't you?" she said anxiously.

The young sleuth agreed, if only to reassure the nervous girl. "Maybe that would be wisest, Lisa."

Nancy concealed her own impatience as the servant went off to the telephone to carry out Lisa's instructions.

Tense moments dragged by while they waited for a scout car to arrive. Several more sounds were heard.

Nancy fretted inwardly that some unknown intruder might be going through the last remaining personal effects of Miss Louise Duval. She herself had come to the Thorpes' house hoping to find in their attic a clue that would help her solve the mystery of Miss Duval's letter to Pierre's grandfather. But someone else may have had the same idea.

At this very moment, the intruder might be

making off with important evidence!

"Lisa, I'm going upstairs and find out who's there," the teenage detective announced abruptly.

"Oh, Nancy! Are you sure that's safe?" Lisa quavered.

"I'll be careful," Nancy promised.

Booker insisted on accompanying her, armed with a flashlight and rolling pin, while Lisa brought up the rear.

The three ascended to the second floor, then quietly opened the attic stairway door. Nancy thought she heard another faint creak of footsteps above, but cautioned the others with a finger to her lips.

The trio now tiptoed hastily up another flight of stairs to the topmost level of the house. From the chilly draft of air on their faces, and the audible patter of rain outside, it was evident that one of the attic windows must be open; otherwise, silence reigned.

Booker switched on his flashlight and shone the bright yellow beam all around. There was no one in sight! However, he checked around carefully among the cluttered items.

Satisfied at last that no housebreaker was crouched in hiding, he went back down to the foot of the stairs and switched on the lights.

With the attic now brightly illuminated, the two girls could see that a casement window was flapping open. But if any intruder had indeed entered this way, they had obviously failed to take him by surprise.

Door chimes sounded from below.

"That must be the police!" Lisa exclaimed in relief. The girls and Booker hurried downstairs to let them in.

The two patrol-car officers who had answered the call wiped their feet carefully and apologized for any tracking. Their uniform slickers were streaming with moisture from the storm.

After accompanying the girls upstairs and looking around, they seemed doubtful that any intruder had broken into the attic.

"Sure you weren't just imagining things?" one policeman said, pushing back his cap and scratching his forehead.

"What we heard certainly *sounded* like footsteps," Lisa said hesitantly.

"This window was open," Nancy pointed out, "and as you can see, it doesn't fit its frame very tightly. Someone could have climbed up that tree just outside and slipped in a knife to open the latch."

"But on a rainy night like this, he sure would have left wet footprints," the officer argued, "and I don't see any around."

Nevertheless, the two policemen promised to report the incident to headquarters and also to scour the neighborhood for any suspicious characters. After they had left, the girls went back upstairs to search for clues to the mystery Nancy was trying to solve.

The attic was crowded with discarded furniture, piles of back-issue magazines, boxes, crates, and old-fashioned luggage. Much of the clutter was furred with dust, but in places the dust had been freshly rubbed away!

"Nancy, this certainly looks as though someone's been up here!" Lisa declared.

The young detective nodded, frowning slightly. "Yes, and I've just realized why there were no wet prints, Lisa. The intruder could have pulled heavy socks over his shoes to avoid tracking, or else simply have taken off his shoes or rubbers before he climbed in."

The distant sound of a door opening and slamming, followed by a voice drifting up from below, indicated that someone had just arrived.

"That must be my father," Lisa murmured. From her pale-wide-eyed expression and sudden nervousness, Nancy realized she was worried over how he might react to her visitor.

Presently Norton Thorpe came stalking up the attic stairs. He stopped short on seeing Nancy Drew and glared at her angrily for a moment. Then with an ill-tempered snort he turned on his tremulous daughter. "Now I *know* you should stay from that worthless, scoundrel of a Frenchman!" Mr. Thorpe declared in a loud, contemptuous voice.

13

Phantom Fashions

Nancy realized at once that Norton Thorpe's rude outburst could refer to only one person, Pierre Michaud. But his choice of words seemed unusually harsh, even for a blustering bully like Thorpe. She wondered what had provoked this latest display of bad temper.

Evidently, so did Lisa. After a moment's hesitation, she murmured, "Daddy, I don't think you've any call to talk that way about Pierre, especially in front of a friend of his."

"Oh, you don't, eh?" her father retorted. His face took on a mockingly sarcastic expression. "Then maybe Miss Drew here hasn't told you the latest news about her pushy young French friend. I just heard it on the car radio, driving home."

"What news, Daddy?" Lisa said anxiously.

"He almost blew himself up while he was showing off his brilliant new invention."

"Oh, no!" Lisa gasped, and a shocked look came over her lovely, ivory-skinned face.

"Don't worry, he wasn't hurt, aside from a few scratches and bruises," Nancy assured her.

"Hmph, too bad. Might've taught the young fool a lesson," grunted Norton Thorpe.

This heartless remark was too much for Nancy. "If you'll forgive my saying so, Mr. Thorpe," she said mildly, "I don't see why Pierre's accident is any reason to dislike or despise him. It doesn't prove anything at all about his character."

"That's what *you* think, young lady. If you were a little older and more experienced, you'd realize it proves a good deal about his character. It shows that he's either a crackpot, who knows nothing about engineering, or else that he's mixed up with a bunch of dangerous foreign crooks who probably followed him over to this country!"

"Actually, Mr. Thorpe, the explosion was due to sabotage," Nancy Drew responded in a calm voice. "There was definite evidence indicating that the computer he was using to demonstrate his device had been bobby-trapped—perhaps because his invention's so good it may outdate other equipment on the market. I know," Nancy added, "because I was there when the blast occurred and discovered the evidence myself."

The heavyset businessman had been about to heap scorn on her defense of Pierre Michaud. But Nancy's last words robbed him of any effective retort and left Thorpe gaping in speechless irritation.

Flushing darkly, he turned to vent his anger on Lisa. "Make up all the excuses for him you like. I say that scheming Frenchman's up to no good! And I trust we've seen the last of him around here!"

Lisa looked pale and nervous, but said bravely, "I think you're being unjust, Father. Pierre may or may not be successful, but it must've taken courage for him to come over here and try to make good in a foreign country with nothing more than faith in his own idea. Personally I think he's an example of what you always call the best American tradition."

Nancy realized that it had also taken courage on Lisa's part to differ with her father. Both girls wondered anxiously how he would react.

Norton Thorpe looked startled at first, then incredulous, as if he could hardly believe his daughter would dare to disagree with him. His face had taken on a scowl like a thundercloud.

But gradually, much to Nancy's and Lisa's relief, his scowl faded and gave way to a new look of grudging respect.

"Hmph! We're all entitled to our own opinions, I suppose," he grumbled. Then he turned and stalked off down the attic stairs, without demanding that Lisa's guest leave the house.

The two girls looked at each other. Lisa rolled her eyes and heaved a soft sigh of relief. "Whew!" Then both laughed quietly.

"Well, come on! Let's see what's up here!" Lisa said with a fresh burst of enthusiasm.

Since the girls did not know exactly what they were looking for, they realized the task might take hours. After all, the jumble of old objects and containers had taken years to accumulate. They could hardly hope to examine it all in a single evening.

Nancy pointed out that any of Louise Duval's effects would no doubt have been packed when the family mansion was sold after her death thirty years ago. Any of Paul and Yvette Duval's possessions, on the other hand, would more likely have been stored over a century and a half ago.

"I'm not sure that helps us much," the pretty young sleuth admitted with a rueful smile. "Still, it may give us a rough guideline."

"I see what you mean, Nancy." Lisa nodded.

"Sounds like a good idea. We'll concentrate on stuff that looks either that old or that recent."

The labels or markings on some of the boxes enabled the girls to judge when they had been packed. Also, in some cases, the contents had been wrapped in newspapers which gave a more exact storage date. Going by such indications, they were able to eliminate a number of items.

Even so, they found themselves searching luggage and crates of family keepsakes, clothing, and household goods that were of no help at all. Some of the stuff looked to be from the period of World War I or World War II; others seemed to date far back into the nineteenth century.

"Fascinating," Nancy sighed as they gave up on yet another box, "but we're still clueless."

"Wait, this looks interesting!" said Lisa, turning to an ancient, brass-bound trunk. "And it must be a hundred years old at the very least!"

"You're right, that's a real antique!" her companion agreed.

A small, brass key was sticking out of the keyhole of the clasp. It turned fairly easily and the clasp sprang open. As Lisa pushed up the trunk lid, its hinges squeaked in protest.

"Oh, Nancy, look! It's full of old gowns!" the

Thorpe girl exclaimed. "Aren't they *beautiful*?"

Nancy caught her breath as Lisa pulled out a lace-trimmed evening gown of shimmering, rose-red taffeta, then a graceful, puff-sleeved chemise dress in classic Grecian style, made of filmy light green muslin.

"They *must* have been Yvette Duval's!" the young detective declared. "At least, the period is right. Those high-waisted styles were popular just around 1800!"

Both girls were thrilled at the thought that these garments had doubtless been worn by the beautiful young woman whose portrait hung in the downstairs hall.

"What a treasure trove!" said Lisa, awestruck as they probed through the contents of the trunk. "To think of these lovely creations being buried away up here all these years!"

Besides the musty assortment of gowns, there were silken petticoats, several scarves, a velvet cloak, long-sleeved gloves, even a satin bonnet.

"How odd!" Nancy murmured as she came on quite a different sort of garment. This was a simple, crudely sewn dress of coarse, dark jersey cloth with a lace-up bodice. It was soiled and stained and seemed the kind of dress that had probably been worn with an apron.

"What on earth is that doing in with all these rich gowns?" Lisa puzzled.

"I'm wondering too," Nancy mused. "It looks more like a dress that a peasant girl or workwoman might have worn."

As Lisa lifted out some of the more beautiful clothes so they could examine the peasant dress, there was a metallic tinkle. Something had struck the trunk clasp while falling to the floor. Nancy bent to pick it up, and gasped.

"It's a gold wedding ring!"

"Is there a name on it?" Lisa asked excitedly.

Nancy held it up to the light and peered at the tiny engraved lettering inside the golden circlet. "Yes, two names," she announced. "*Yvette* and *Philippe*. And the year *1789*."

"*Phillipe?*" Lisa echoed with a puzzled frown. "Are you sure?"

"See for yourself." Nancy handed her the ring.

Lisa studied its engraving under the light, then looked at her friend in perplexity. "I don't understand. Her husband's name was Paul, not Philippe."

Nancy responded with a thoughtful nod. "I know. In fact there's outside evidence to confirm that fact." She told about the old newspaper article discovered by Mr. Teakin of the historical society, which referred to Paul and Yvette Duval by name. "Perhaps your ancestress was married twice," the teenage sleuth suggested.

"I suppose that's possible," Lisa said, her forehead still puckered in a slight frown. "But if so, it's strange that the family was never aware of it . . . or if they were, that it was completely forgotten. Still, I guess all memories fade with time, don't they?"

The storm had let up when Nancy left the Thorpes' house soon afterward. She sensed that this was only a temporary lull, and hoped she could reach home before the downpour resumed. Unhappily, she had driven only a few blocks when a fresh gust of rain struck her windshield.

Oh, what luck! she thought wryly. Now I'll probably get drenched before I get indoors again!

She slowed at a blinking-light intersection and peered both ways. The streets seemed deserted at this late hour, and no one was coming from either direction. But as she started across, Nancy glanced in her rearview mirror, then reacted as if she had received an electric shock.

A big, old-fashioned red car was following her—from all appearances, the same car that had chased her the other night!

And, as before, Nancy could make out no driver at the wheel!

A pang of fear shot through the girl! She trod hard on the gas pedal to increase speed, even though she sensed already that her pursuer meant to dog her trail relentlessly!

Sure enough, the red car, too, speeded up. The empty blackness of its front seat was terrifying. But Nancy soon had other problems to claim her attention. The road wound steeply downhill toward the neighborhood where the Drews lived. And steering her car was becoming more and more difficult.

What had happened to her power steering? She could hardly turn the wheel. Nancy hesitated to apply the brakes with her ghostly pursuer so close behind. But she knew she would have to do so soon, unless she could bring her car under control. Otherwise she was in danger of going off the road!

Almost in the same moment that the thought crossed Nancy's mind, the decision was taken out of her hands!

There was a sudden *thumpety-bump-bump!* as her right wheel hit the curb. Her car slued and bounded from the paved road surface onto the dirt shoulder!

The shock jolted Nancy half out of her seat. She uttered a frozen scream of fright as she glimpsed the steep hillside yawning across her field of vision.

The next instant her car went skidding and crashing down the rough, brush-covered hillside!

14

Legal Threats

Using all of her strength, Nancy wrestled with the steering wheel as it jerked and twisted first in one direction, then in the other. All the while on her wild ride down the hillside, she was trying to stop the car by pushing on the brake pedal. Finally, when she thought she could do no more, she was able to bring the car to a halt, still upright and in one piece.

Considerably shaken and weak, Nancy leaned her head on the steering wheel while the storm raged on.

"Whew!" she said as she pulled herself together, opened the door, and stepped out into the rain.

"I guess the thing to do is to walk back up to the road and down to the next public phone," she muttered to herself as she climbed up the hillside, rain streaming over her from head to feet.

Walking as fast as she could against the storm, she reached the shelter of the phone booth and called one of the 24-hour towing service numbers provided by the company that insured her car. Nancy explained her predicament and asked if she could be dropped off at her house while the car was being towed to Bill's Garage, where the Drews were old customers.

"Sure, no problem," the service man said cheerfully, "if you don't mind riding up in the cab with me."

Twenty minutes later, Nancy walked into her house, drenched to the skin. The rest of the household was asleep, and Nancy, after disposing of her wet clothes, dried her hair and left a note for her father explaining what had happened to her car. Then she fell into bed exhausted.

She was so tired that she slept later than usual the next morning. By the time she showered and dressed, it was after 9:30 A.M.

Going downstairs, she found a place set for her at the kitchen table and a note from Hannah saying she had gone to the supermarket. Carson Drew had long since left for the office, so Nancy sat down to a lonely breakfast.

On the way to the refrigerator for milk and orange juice, Nancy switched on a small TV set that Hannah kept on the kitchen counter.

"May as well listen to the news," she said as she settled down at the table and spooned some strawberries onto her cereal.

"And now for some local news items," the announcer's voice boomed out. "Here in River Heights, artists and other participants in the local art scene were shocked by the revelation that the prize-winning painting in a recent art contest was a copy of a picture owned by the River Heights Museum. The discovery that artist Lee Talbot had copied his subject matter from the work of another painter was made by the famous teenage detective, Nancy Drew. Talbot could not be reached for . . ."

Nancy, very upset, switched off the TV set and went into the living room to look at the copy of the *Morning Record*, which had been brought in earlier from the porch by Carson Drew. Hastily checking through the paper, Nancy found the story of the copied painting on page 3. But this report made no mention of her part in the affair.

Puzzled, Nancy went into the hall to the telephone and quickly dialed the newspaper office. She asked to speak to reporter Peter Worden.

"Hello, Nancy," he said when she reached him. "You read my story in the *Morning Record*, right?"

"Yes, I did, Peter. Thank you for not mentioning my name."

"I always try to grant the request of beautiful girls," the reporter answered flirtatiously.

Nancy laughed. "Even though you didn't publish it, did you *mention* my name to anyone in connection with the story?"

"Absolutely not," he said in a more serious voice. "Why do you ask?"

"I was just listening to the morning news on television," Nancy replied. "The broadcast named me as the one who discovered that Lee Talbot's painting was a copy."

"Well, I'll be!" Peter Worden exclaimed. "Nancy, I don't know what to say. I swear I didn't violate your confidence. I told nobody." He declared this so earnestly and sounded so distressed that Nancy could not help but believe him.

"It's certainly a puzzle," she said in a troubled voice, "and it leaves me in a very unpleasant position. Still, there's no use fretting over it—what's done is done. I suppose sooner or later we'll find out how my name was brought into it."

"I'll check around and see what I can find out, Nancy," Worden said unhappily. "Meanwhile, if I can help in any way, please call on me."

Thanking him, Nancy returned to her unfinished breakfast in the kitchen. But the sight of the soggy cereal in the bowl drove away what little appetite she had left. Just then, the telephone rang and Nancy went to answer it.

"Miss Nancy Drew, please. Emily Owsler calling."

"This is Nancy speaking, Miss Owsler. How are you?"

"Oh—I'm just fine, dear." The maid paused as if to choose her next words, then went on. "I've just thought of something of Miss Duval's that might help you, something I was given as a keepsake. Perhaps you would like to look at it?"

Nancy's mood brightened. "Yes, indeed, Miss Owsler. Er, what is it?"

"An old photograph album. I thought by looking at the pictures in it, you might come across a clue of some sort," the elderly woman said hopefully.

"Why, that's an excellent idea! Thanks ever so much for letting me know."

Nancy arranged to visit Miss Owsler. She had no sooner hung up and turned away than the telephone shrilled again.

"I'd like to speak to Nancy Drew," snarled an angry voice.

"I'm Nancy Drew. Who is this?"

"This, Miss Drew, is Lee Talbot. You have

publicly and falsely accused me of stealing, of plagiarism. I am therefore suing you for libel and defamation of character. You'll hear from my lawyer!" he threatened.

A look of dismay flickered over Nancy's face during this stormy speech. But she replied calmly enough, "Then please have your attorney contact my father, Carson Drew. He will act as my counsel."

Lee Talbot's response was to slam down the receiver, breaking the connection.

As Nancy turned from the phone, Hannah Gruen, the Drews' housekeeper, bustled in the door with two bags of groceries.

On seeing Nancy's expression, Hannah asked, "Has anything happened, dear? You look very upset and unhappy." She gave the girl a quick hug after setting down her load from the supermarket.

"Oh, Hannah, I've had a rather unpleasant morning. Could you take time out and drive me to Bill's Garage so I can pick up my car? I'll tell you all my troubles on the way."

They reached the garage in the Drews' station wagon just as Nancy finished relating the morning's events, ending with a description of Lee Talbot's threatening telephone call.

"My goodness, no wonder you looked so upset, dear!" a worried Hannah exclaimed as

Nancy got out of the car. "But don't let it get you down. I'm sure your father will know how to deal with that fellow. In the meantime, take care of yourself."

"I'll try, Hannah. Good-bye and thanks for the lift."

Rick, the garage mechanic, was just closing the hood of Nancy's car. "All set, Miss Drew," he smiled, then added more soberly, "I think you ought to be more careful where you park your car, hereafter."

"Oh? Why?"

"Some joker cut the power steering hose. All the fluid leaked out."

"So that's why I had so much trouble turning the wheel!" Nancy frowned reflectively. "At first I didn't notice anything wrong. But I suppose the fluid leaked out gradually as I drove along."

"Right. Also, another odd thing, we had a call this morning. Fellow wanting to know if we had picked up Nancy Drew's car."

As Nancy's eyes widened, Rick said. "Maybe you ought to report it to the police."

"You're right, I will," the girl sleuth promised. She paid the repair bill and drove off.

Nancy decided to check with the curator at the art museum to try to find out how her name got into the news report about Lee Talbot's painting. But when she saw him in his office later that morning, he was unable to shed any light on the matter.

"No one talked to me about Lee Talbot or his painting, Nancy," Mr. Gregory said regretfully. "I'm sorry I can't help."

Seeing her disappointed look, however, he went on, hoping to cheer her up.

"But we *have* located that missing picture you were asking about—the one donated by the Duval family when the museum first opened!"

15

An Odd Likeness

Mr. Gregory opened the door to a closet in his
office and brought out a painting with an old,
ornate gilt frame. Nancy stared at the portrait.

The painter had depicted a handsome young
man with dark eyes and a cleft chin. He was
dressed in the elegant style of the late eight-
eenth century. He had a tall, white powdered
wig and a pale blue velvet coat embroidered in
gold with a frothy jabot gathered at the throat of
his fine white shirt.

"A striking fellow, I must admit," Mr. Gregory remarked, "even if the painting's not all that
valuable."

"Yes," Nancy agreed and went on musingly,
"It's strange, but he reminds me of someone."
Try as she would, Nancy could not place the

143

resemblance. "Can you tell me anything about the painting, Mr. Gregory, besides the fact that it was donated by the Duval family?"

The curator pointed to some small, scriptlike markings in the lower right-hand corner of the canvas. "Well, I have deciphered the artist's signature. He was Antoine Grivet, a minor French painter who flourished in the late 1700s. The date is less easy to make out, but appears to be 1790."

"Is there any way to find out whose portrait this was?" Nancy asked.

"Hm, yes, it may be possible to establish the subject of the picture. One would have to consult an expert who specializes in French art of that period. There's a chap in New York who might be able to help. I'll call him this afternoon."

Mr. Gregory replaced the painting in the closet and locked the door, then glanced at his watch. "Oh, my goodness. I have a meeting with the trustees in five minutes. Nancy, could you excuse me?"

"Of course. And thanks ever so much for letting me know about the Duval painting."

"A pleasure, my dear. It's the least I could do after your efforts to help solve those break-ins."

They parted outside the curator's office. Mr. Gregory bustled off down the corridor. As

Nancy walked toward the marble staircase which led down into the lobby, she happened to glance in an open doorway. A dark-haired young woman in a blue smock was bent over a framed painting on a worktable in front of her, carefully examining and cleaning the painted canvas. The young woman looked up and their eyes met.

"Hi, Nancy!" She was the curator's assistant, Jane Heron. "On the trail of another mystery?"

"Well, a small one." Nancy paused for a moment to chat. "But so far I'm not having much luck."

"What's the mystery, may I ask?"

"How that television news report this morning came to name me as the one who discovered that Lee Talbot's prize-winning painting looked like a picture in the museum."

"But you *are* the one, aren't you?"

Nancy smiled ruefully. "Yes and no. Actually it was a reporter for the *Record*, Peter Worden, who first noticed the similarity. I just happened to spot the picture he had in mind. It was the one I photographed down in the basement storage area, remember?"

Miss Heron nodded, looking troubled. "Yes, indeed I do."

"But, you see, I knew the discovery was likely to stir up a good deal of unpleasantness, and I didn't want to become involved. So I asked Mr. Worden not to mention my name when he wrote his news story. He promised he wouldn't, and he assures me he kept his promise. Yet the television newscaster this morning named me as the person who made the discovery."

"Oh, dear!" A look of distress had come over Jane Heron's face. "Nancy, I'm very much afraid that I'm the one who's to blame!"

"You?" Nancy stared at the museum staffer in surprise. "I don't understand. How did it happen?"

Miss Heron explained unhappily that a television camera crew had come to the museum to photograph the picture in question, after picking up Worden's story over the news wire, even before it appeared in the morning *Record*.

"They wanted to interview me," she went on, "but at the time I knew nothing about the matter, so all I could tell them was that I had seen you photographing the picture. They must have assumed from that that you were the one who'd discovered the similarity of the two paintings."

The girl detective responded with a thoughtful nod. "Yes, that probably explains it."

"Oh, Nancy, I'm terribly sorry!" Jane Heron exclaimed, reaching out to squeeze her hand. "I just wasn't using my head. I should have spoken to you before mentioning your name. Can you possibly forgive me for not being more cautious?"

Seeing that the woman was upset, Nancy summoned a smile. "Don't worry, you had no way of knowing. In your place, I might have done the same. At least you've solved one mystery for me."

After leaving the museum, Nancy decided to visit Pierre Michaud, to see how he was coming along repairing his invention, and also to tell him about the latest developments in his case.

When she arrived at his workshop, she found him busily at work with his tools and electronic equipment. "You see, Nancy, a representative of the National Computer Company called and said they were interested in seeing my memory device. So I must have everything ready to demonstrate my invention when he comes here. He may be in River Heights within the next day or two."

"Golly, can you be ready that soon?"

"*Oui*, if that is when he is coming, then I *must* be ready, even if it means working day and night," Pierre replied with a smile. "Anything is possible if one works hard enough! Is that not what you say here in America?"

Watching his mobile features while he talked, Nancy was struck by a sudden realization. Now she knew whom the man in the portrait reminded her of! No doubt the wig had thrown her off.

"Is something wrong?" Pierre inquired, seeing her startled expression.

Nancy's blue eyes twinkled. "Far from it. In fact you just made something come right for me." She described the picture which the museum curator had shown her and asked if by any chance it might be a painting of someone in his family.

"*Mais non*, Nancy. It could not be a Michaud. My family was of humble origin. No velvet or gold-embroidered clothes for us!" He laughed and added with a wave of his hand toward the computer assembly. "There may be before long, though, if I can get this finished and sell it!"

Nancy was about to leave a short time later when an expensive-looking car pulled up outside the building and Pierre's backer, Mr. Varney, came striding into the workshop. The big, vigorous-looking financier seemed preoccupied and disturbed.

"My boy," he blurted, "I don't like the way things are shaping up, not one bit."

"Do you mean the explosion, sir?" Pierre asked anxiously.

"Not only the blast itself, but the news report that was broadcast about what happened. Do you realize this could ruin your chances of selling your invention? Nobody wants to invest in something so risky it may blow up in his face!"

"But, Mr. Varney, you were here just after it happened. You know the explosion was not my fault. Miss Drew will tell you that the computer I was using to demonstrate my device had been bobby-trapped. Some enemy wired it with a bomb that was set to go off when the computer was turned on!"

"Yes, yes, *we* know all that. But that is certainly not the impression that listeners to the news broadcast will get. I'm sorry, but I may have to reconsider giving you any further financial support!"

Pierre's face was glum. "I hope you will not decide too hastily, sir, now that my work has progressed this far. In spite of the accident, another computer manufacturer is also interested in my memory device."

The young Frenchman told his backer about the call which he had already mentioned to Nancy. Then, pacing about the workshop with a worried expression, Pierre went on, "I will admit, sir, I was quite upset myself about that news broadcast. I only wish I could find out who circulated the story. I even called the radio station, but they could tell me nothing."

"But they must have gotten their information *somewhere*," put in Nancy. "Wouldn't they reveal their source?"

"They said only that someone had phoned the story to their news desk. The person who took it down simply assumed the call came from one of the news services to which the station subscribes."

Nancy frowned. "Obviously you have an enemy, Pierre. The caller must have been someone who's trying to stop you from selling your invention."

Mr. Varney, with a look of alarm, said, "For your own safety's sake, my boy, maybe you ought to stop work for a while. Or perhaps move to another area."

"But I am already set up here in River Heights, sir. Why should I leave when my work is progressing so well?"

The financier pursed his lips and frowned. "At least think about it. I'll let you know my own decision soon." With a nod to both Nancy and Pierre, Varney left and drove away.

Nancy, seeing that Pierre had a great deal on

his mind in addition to his pressing work schedule, left soon afterward with a few parting words of encouragement. She drove to her father's office.

Nancy gave a sigh of relief as she entered his comfortable private sanctum with its deep leather chairs, polished dark wood, and wall-wide shelves filled with law books.

"Why, Nancy! This is a nice surprise." Carson Drew rose from behind his desk to give her a hug and a kiss.

"Thanks for letting me barge in on you, Dad. I've had such an upsetting morning! And I need some good legal advice."

"Well, tell your old dad all about it. Then we'll go and have a nice lunch." Mr. Drew waited until Nancy was comfortably seated, then settled down to listen.

It was a relief to Nancy to tell her father about her accidental involvement in the prize painting dispute. She had just finished describing the angry call she had received during breakfast from Lee Talbot when the phone on Mr. Drew's desk rang.

He picked it up, listened for a moment as his secretary told of someone on the line, and said he would take the call.

"Carson Drew here . . . Oh yes, Counsellor

... Hm. Well, why don't we meet here in my office at 3:30 this afternoon? If you care to bring your client, I'll have my daughter here at that time and we can discuss the matter ... Very well, sir. See you at 3:30."

Mr. Drew hung up and looked at Nancy. "That was Aaron Locke, Lee Talbot's lawyer. You're being sued for libel."

16

The French Imposter

Nancy gasped in dismay on hearing about the lawsuit. But Carson Drew merely smiled at his daughter.

"Come now, don't be upset. I think a good lunch is just what you need. Let's go."

"Okay, Dad," Nancy said, accompanying him out the office door. "You know, I think I'm as angry at Lee Talbot as I am worried."

Mr Drew chuckled. "Good! But don't let it interfere with your appetite."

They were soon seated in the quiet, oak-beamed, English-style restaurant that Carson Drew favored for its good food and efficient service.

Nancy was so hungry that she tucked into her eggs Benedict and listened to her father discuss one of his interesting cases. When dessert arrived and he saw that she was in better spirits, he changed the subject.

"Now let me tell you about a visit I had this morning concerning Pierre Michaud." Carson Drew paused to take a sip of coffee as Nancy looked up from her French pastry with keen interest.

"A visit? . . . From whom?"

"Fellow said his name was Henri Grison. A French lawyer."

"What did he want, Dad?" Nancy asked.

"Information about Pierre. Did I know him? Where was he staying? What was he doing here in the United States? Anything and everything he could pry out of me."

"How much did you tell him?"

"Exactly nothing, except that I'd met the young man in question." Carson Drew took a forkful of apple pie.

"I wonder what he was after," Nancy mused aloud.

"Precisely what I asked him after he finished trying to pump me for information," Mr. Drew replied.

"Yes?" Nancy prompted.

"He said Pierre was an unsavory character, out to cheat people out of their money—a con man, in fact. He claimed to have followed Pierre's trail from Paris to this country. But he never did give me a straight answer to my question regarding his own interest in Pierre Michaud."

Carson Drew reached into his pocket and took out a business card, which he handed to Nancy. "So after he left my office, I called one of my French legal colleagues, gave him the address on the card, and asked him to check out Grison."

"Has he reported back yet?"

"Yes, just a few minutes before you showed up in my office. He told me there's no attorney at that address, and no such person as Henri Grison even practicing law in Paris."

Somehow Nancy was not too surprised at this news. Suddenly she had an inspiration. Could Henri Grison be the menacing thug who had been following her, and who had lain in wait for her outside the house the other night?

"Dad, was Grison a rather tough-looking, swarthy man with thick, dark eyebrows and sort of a heavy jut jaw?"

"Doesn't sound much like him. This fellow was a tall man, slightly balding, with glasses."

Nancy sighed and smiled. "I guess this isn't my day."

While her father was finishing his coffee,

Nancy excused herself to call Police Chief McGinnis from the telephone booth in the restaurant's lounge.

"Chief McGinnis, this is Nancy Drew. I won't keep you but a minute. May I ask a favor?"

"Any time, Nancy. Just fire away."

The teenage detective related the details of Louise Duval's death thirty years ago.

"Would you please check the police files to see if there was any report of foul play in connection with her heart attack? I mean, did her maid or doctor call in to report that it was brought on by a red car trying to run her down? And if so, was there any follow-up investigation?"

"Hm." The police chief paused to consider for a moment. "That may not be too easy, Nancy. I'm not sure how complete our files would be, going that far back. But I'll see what I can find out and let you know if I turn up anything."

After thanking him, Nancy hung up.

The Drews walked back to the law office together and Nancy said good-bye. "I really feel a lot better, Dad," she said cheerfully as they parted. "See you at 3:30."

Nancy got into her car, keyed the ignition, and swung out into traffic. She was going to keep her promise to drop by Emily Owsler's apartment.

Gradually, she became aware that she was being followed. But this time it was not a big, old-fashioned red car. It was a smaller, dark green one. To make sure her imagination wasn't working overtime, Nancy pulled over to the curb as if for a closer look at some dresses on display in a shop window. Sure enough, the shadow car too came to a stop down the block. And as Nancy drove away, the dark green car also pulled out from the curb again to follow her.

Nancy decided on a plan. A minute or two later, after passing a gas station, she stopped for a second time, pulling over to the curb abruptly just past the service station driveway. Taking out her compact, she pretended to check on her hair and makeup. But as the dark green car went by, she noted the license plate number and studied its driver in her compact mirror.

He was the swarthy snoop she had just described to her father!

Closing her purse, Nancy quickly backed around into the gas station driveway, then sped off in the opposite direction. After zigzagging back and forth for a number of blocks, she felt confident that she had shaken off her pursuer.

Before reaching Emily Owsler's home, however, Nancy stopped at a corner phone booth and called Chief McGinnis.

"Sorry to bother you again," she apologized, "but I'm being followed by a man in a dark green car. If I give you his license plate number, could you check it out, please?"

"Sure thing, Nancy. I'll let you know as soon as I have any information."

Nancy finished the trip to Emily Owsler's apartment and rang the doorbell, wondering if her visit would prove a waste of time. One look at Miss Owsler's happy face, however, was a more than sufficient answer, in one respect at least. The lonely old woman obviously enjoyed having company and was delighted at the chance to become involved in something exciting.

"Oh, Nancy, I do hope you can get a clue from this album!" she said, leading the way into her tiny, crowded living room.

"We both hope so," Nancy responded with a smile.

"I keep it in this closet," Miss Owsler went on, opening a door in one corner of the room.

The closet contained a few coats and jackets and an umbrella. On a shelf above the rack lay a thick, old black book with a hat on top of it. Emily Owsler reached up with both hands. But as she tried to hold the hat and take down the book, she lost her grip on the heavy album and it fell to the floor. A folded, yellowing sheet of parchment spilled out from between its pages.

"Oh dear, how clumsy of me," Miss Owsler quavered.

Nancy picked up the album and glanced at the parchment, which had come open. Suddenly her eyes sparkled with excitement. "Why, it's an old letter," she exclaimed, "written in French!"

Even more important, Nancy saw at a glance, it began with the words *Ma chère Yvette*!

17

A Tantalizing Translation

Nancy understood French and could hardly wait to read the letter. Miss Owsler insisted that the young sleuth sit down and make herself comfortable on the overstuffed sofa, while she went to the kitchen and made them some tea.

As the elderly woman bustled off to the kitchen, Nancy eagerly perused the letter. It was dated March 23, 1797, from Brighton, England.

> *Dear Yvette,*
> *I must write in haste in order that this letter may go aboard the mail packet before it sails. I regret to report that all our efforts have still failed to find your precious lost treasure so unhappily left behind by force of circumstance when you crossed the Channel from France three*

*years ago. Wartime turmoil renders our
search ever more difficult, but do not de-
spair! Our efforts will continue without
cease! Meanwhile, my husband and I send
our best wishes and hopes that you and
Paul may find happiness in your new
home in the United States.*

Your loving sister,
Charlotte

As she finished reading the letter, Nancy's
thoughts raced back to last night's scene in the
Thorpes' attic, when she and Lisa had found
Yvette's wedding ring. Nancy was now more
convinced than ever that her guess was right
about Yvette's having been wed twice. If she
had lived in France before marrying Paul,
perhaps her previous marriage had occured in
that country, and her husband, Philippe, had
died there before her crossing to England.

But what was the "lost treasure" referred to
in the letter? And what had Louise Duval found
out about it? Was that what the present mystery
was all about, and what the various unknown
parties in this case were hunting for?

Nancy barely had time to consider these
questions when Miss Owsler came back with
tea things on a tray.

"Now, dear, we'll have a nice cup of tea
while we look through the album," she said.

As they sat side by side on the sofa sipping their tea, with Miss Owsler turning the pages and commenting on the snapshots and other photographs, Nancy's thoughts were still occupied with the letter. She scarcely noticed the pictures as the former maid pointed them out.

But suddenly the woman exclaimed triumphantly. She was pointing to a photo of Louise Duval standing with a man in front of a building that looked like an old gristmill, of the kind still found in the Northeastern states.

"That's him!" Emily Owsler cried. "That's the man Miss Duval hired to do the research for her that summer just before she passed away! I remember his face now."

"Oh, wonderful!" Nancy could hardly believe her good luck, but realized she had better not congratulate herself too soon without more to go on. "Does seeing his picture by any chance remind you of his name?"

"Oh dear . . . let me see now." The elderly woman thought hard, then shook her head, looking crestfallen. "I'm afraid not," she confessed, smiling wistfully. "I seem to have a hard time remembering names these days."

"My goodness, don't worry about that," Nancy said with a gentle laugh. "So does everybody at some time or other. What about the place, though? That building looks like an

163

old mill. Have you any idea where the picture may have been taken?"

Again Emily Owsler raked her memory but was forced to give up. "No, I'm afraid not, dear," she said, shaking her head regretfully.

"Never mind, Miss Owsler. You've been a tremendous help! Would you mind letting me borrow this picture for a day or two? I'll be very careful with it."

"Yes, of course. Do take it. I hope it will help you solve your mystery case." And Emily Owsler began carefully peeling the glued photo from the album page.

After thanking the woman for the tea and the valuable discoveries they had just made, Nancy returned to her blue sports car parked in the street below.

She was eager to show the snapshot to Professor Crawford's daughter. But remembering the 3:30 appointment at her dad's office with Lee Talbot and his attorney, Nancy curbed her impatience and turned her car toward the law office.

Driving along Main Street, she decided to stop at the River Heights Camera Shop and pick up her developed roll of film and pictures. They included an enlarged print of her photograph of the museum's painting.

164

With this safely in her purse, Nancy drove to the appointment in a slightly more confident frame of mind.

The teenage sleuth arrived at the office only moments after Lee Talbot and his lawyer had appeared. The artist, elegantly dressed as always, was so angry he was barely civil. Ignoring his rude manner, Carson Drew introduced Nancy to Talbot's small, sharp-featured attorney, and they all sat down.

Brushing aside Mr. Drew's efforts to set out the facts clearly and without bias, Aaron Locke belligerently began telling the Drews that Nancy had grievously wronged Lee Talbot and besmirched his reputation and character, and that the only problem to be resolved was how much should be paid to his client in damages.

"Well now, before we get to that," Carson Drew's voice cut incisively through Locke's blustering speech, "let's get a few preliminary facts straight. What exactly does Mr. Talbot have to say regarding this alleged resemblance of his prize-winning painting to the picture in the museum?"

Lee Talbot glared haughtily at the distinguished lawyer. "I have nothing to say, sir! I've been to our local museum, naturally, and I may have seen the picture in question at some time or other. Perhaps there may even be some slight superficial resemblance. But any allegation of copying is ridiculous!"

"Very well, you've heard my client's answer," Aaron Locke said in a hard voice. "Now then, are you going to settle . . ."

Before he could go any further, Nancy took the enlarged photograph of the museum painting out of her shoulder bag. Without a word, she handed it to Lee Talbot and his lawyer, who were sitting next to each other.

No words were needed. At sight of the photograph, the blond artist's mouth dropped open in shocked surprise, and the look on his lawyer's face froze in dismay. It was clear from their expressions that both had instantly realized how suspiciously alike the two painting were!

Nancy said quietly, "Of course I've said nothing yet to the police, Lee. But when they see the evidence, they might get the idea you had a motive for those museum break-ins . . . in other words, that you were trying to remove or destroy the original painting that would prove your plagiarism."

Lee Talbot's face had turned sickly pale. Nancy had chosen her words carefully, to see how he would respond. But his reaction had already convinced her that the artist was innocent and had not deliberately copied the museum work. More likely he had seen the picture at some time in the past, and its composition had impressed him so much that the image had lodged deep in his memory, and then emerged again in his own painting without conscious intent.

Talbot looked helplessly at Aaron Locke, who by now had lost all of his own bluster and aggressiveness. Both were silent, obviously at a loss for words.

Carson Drew stepped into the void. "Perhaps, Mr. Locke, you'd like time to consult with your client?"

The other attorney cleared his throat. "Tell you what, Counsellor. I'll call you tomorrow morning. Perhaps we can work something out." Aaron Locke had recovered his facade.

But Lee Talbot looked steadily at him, then at Nancy's father and said, "No, Mr. Drew. We won't be calling you. I don't want—"

Locke hastily interrupted, "Now, now! We'll talk before coming to any decision." And, both having risen, he hustled the artist out the door.

Carson Drew smiled at Nancy. "I don't think we'll hear any more threats from those two. Congratulations! You handled that beautifully."

Nancy drove her father home that afternoon with a considerably lighter heart. She was looking forward to helping Hannah with dinner and was just putting on an apron in the kitchen when the phone rang. She answered it and heard the kindly baritone voice of Police Chief McGinnis.

"Hi, Nancy. Chief McGinnis here. I have a trace on that license number you gave me. The car belongs to a rental agency, and their records show it was signed out to a French tourist, a man named André Freneau."

Nancy felt a thrill of satisfaction. At last she had identified her swarthy shadow! "I don't suppose you'd know if he has any criminal record?"

"That's the next step, Nancy. I've already put through a request for information on him to Interpol. But it may take time. I'll get back to you as soon as I learn anything."

After thanking the police chief, Nancy went back to her salad making. She had no sooner finished washing the lettuce and the escarole when the telephone rang again.

"I'll get it, Hannah," Nancy said, drying her hands. "I've a feeling it's for me, anyway."

She was right. The caller was Mr. Gregory, the museum curator.

"I've just had a talk with that New York art expert I mentioned, Nancy," Mr. Gregory reported. "He's a specialist in French art of the period around 1800. In his opinion, our museum painting by Antoine Grivet is almost certainly a portrait of a French nobleman, the Comte d'Auvergne!"

18

The Old Gowns

The next morning was a brisk, sunshiny day.
Nancy was delighted when she looked out the
window. She was already intending to drive to
the little crossroads village of Alton, where Professor Crawford's daughter lived, and show her
the snapshot from Louise Duval's album.
Today would be perfect for her drive into the
country!

After breakfast, she telephoned Bess Marvin
to invite her to come along.

"Oh gee, Nancy, I can't! I have an appointment with the dentist," Bess lamented. "But
George is here. Want to ask her?"

"Yes, great! I was going to call her next, anyhow, so we could make it a threesome."

After a few minutes' talk with an eager

George, Nancy arranged to pick her up at Bess's place in fifteen minutes. "Oh, and George," Nancy added, "please ask Bess to meet us here at my house for lunch when we get back. Then we can all have a good chat."

Bess had already left to keep her appointment when Nancy parked in front of the Marvins' house. George came running out of the door, her coat and scarf flying in the wind, before Nancy could turn off the engine.

"Golly, what fun!" George said breathlessly as she jumped into the car and slammed the door. "The woods'll be beautiful, with the leaves all turning! By the way, what're we going to investigate today?"

Nancy told her. "But first I have to stop at Westmoor U.," she added, "and talk to Professor Schmidt in the history department."

When they reached the university, the two girls left Nancy's car in the visitors' parking lot and walked to the professor's office. They found him checking through a pile of exam papers.

"How can I help you, Miss Drew?" he asked genially, taking out his tobacco pouch to fill his pipe after Nancy had said hello and introduced her friend.

"Last time I was here, you told me Professor

171

Crawford specialized in the history of the French Revolution and the Napoleonic Wars. Is that your field, too?"

"Not exactly." Schmidt paused to light his pipe. "I do teach a course in that period of French history, but I certainly can't claim to be as expert in it as Dr. Crawford was. My own specialty is the Third Republic, roughly a century later. Why do you ask?"

"I was wondering what, if anything, you could tell me about a French nobleman who lived during that earlier period, the Comte d'Auvergne. Do you recognize the name?" Nancy asked.

"Hm, d'Auvergne." The professor tapped his pipestem against his lips reflectively. "I don't. But I tell you what, if it's important, I'll check with some of my colleagues at other universities. I could phone them this morning. Would that do?"

"Oh, Professor, I'd really appreciate it if you could," Nancy replied. "Anything you can find out might help in solving a mystery case that I'm working on. Should I call you this afternoon?"

"If you have a phone number that I can reach you at, it might be better to let me call you. I have classes all afternoon and a department meeting this evening."

"In that case, I'll give you my home number,"

Nancy said, jotting it down. "And thanks ever so much for your help!"

She and George were soon on their way. The roadside trees were aflame with fall colors of red and orange and gold, and both girls thoroughly enjoyed the scenery.

"Whom are you going to see in Alton, Nancy?" George asked.

"Professor Crawford's married daughter. As I told you, Louise Duval hired him to carry out some sort of research for her, apparently during his summer vacation thirty years ago. But she died soon afterward, and now of course he's gone too. And so far as I know, the results of his research were never disclosed."

Nancy took her eyes off the road long enough to shoot a mischievous glance at her companion and added, "Incidentally, I've a hunch I'm not the only one who'd like to lay hands on it."

George gave a slight, nervous shudder. "You know something? That sounds pretty sinister!"

"Yes, it does, doesn't it."

The girls arrived shortly at Mrs. Grale's home.

"Come in, come in, Nancy," she said, wiping her hands on a towel she was holding. "I've just been cleaning out some closets and now I'm ready for a coffee break, so you and your friend are just in time."

Leading the way into the kitchen, she went

on, "I just want to get this coffee cake out of the oven, and we can have some of it while we visit."

Soon all three were comfortably seated in the sunny living room. As they sipped their coffee, Nancy took the snapshot from the album out of her bag and handed it to Mrs. Grale. "Does this mean anything to you?"

Mrs. Grale studied the photo and smiled reminiscently. "Oh my, yes. That's my father with that woman you mentioned—um—Miss Duval. I think I even remember when this was taken."

"Then you recognize the location?"

"Oh yes, of course. That's my father's retreat . . . it's an old gristmill near Peachtown. He fell in love with the place and bought it and restored it. He used to go there and write . . . textbooks, you know, and articles for historical journals."

George asked to see the snapshot and admired the old mill in the background. "What happened to it?" she asked.

"Why, it's still standing. It belongs to me now, but I let the historical society there use it as a tourist attraction."

"Since Miss Duval was photographed there with your father," Nancy said, keeping her fingers crossed, "do you suppose there's a chance that any of his research reports might still be there?"

Mrs. Grale wrinkled her forehead thoughtfully as she offered the girls more coffee cake. "Do you know, that's an idea!" she mused. "Come to think of it, my father's old desk is still there. It's on the upper floor of the mill, where he did his working and reading. And I'm almost certain there were papers still in the drawers last time I looked. Just odds and ends, though—I doubt if there's anything important."

"Would you mind if I visited the mill and checked out the desk?" Nancy asked. "I might find a clue to whatever research he was doing for Miss Duval."

"Of course you may," Mrs. Grale answered unhesitatingly. "I'll lend you a key and phone ahead to the Peachtown Historical Society to let them know you're coming. They're in charge of the mill and watch over it," she added, smiling.

Elated and hopeful, Nancy and George chatted a while longer with Mrs. Grale, then left after thanking her for the refreshments and all her help.

Bess was waiting eagerly when the two girls walked into the Drews' house an hour or so later. "Yikes, I thought I'd faint with hunger!" she said. "All those delicious smells coming out of the kitchen . . ."

Nancy laughed. "Well, let's wash our hands and tell Hannah we're home. Then I'll set the table."

"No need to, I did it already," Bess said. Then as George burst out laughing, she added defensively, "Well, it took my mind off the food."

While the three friends enjoyed Hannah's seafood quiche and a green salad, Nancy brought them up to date on the details of the case.

As she told them about the trunkful of old gowns in Lisa's attic, Bess was ecstatic. "Ooh, I'd love to see them!" she cried. "And just think, Nancy—if Yvette Duval *was* a spy, maybe that old peasant dress was one of her disguises!"

Nancy was struck by her friend's idea. "You know, Bess," she murmured thoughtfully, "you might have something there."

Just then the phone rang. When Nancy answered it, her caller turned out to be Professor Schmidt, reporting back on what he had found out about the Comte d'Auvergne.

"He was a wealthy French nobleman who served briefly in the National Assembly during the opening days of the Revolution, when they were writing a new constitution for France. But a few years later he died on the guillotine."

"The guillotine?" Nancy echoed in a shocked voice. "How horrible!" She recalled the handsome young man portrayed in the museum portrait and shuddered to think of him suffering such a fate.

"It was a bad time, you know," Professor Schmidt went on. "The Reign of Terror, they called it. Thousands of people ended up the same way, especially aristocrats like the count."

Nancy thanked him for his help and hung up, still shaken by what he had told her. Then, on a sudden impulse, she called Lisa Thorpe.

After they had chatted for a few moments, Nancy said, "I don't want to sound too hopeful, Lisa, but there's a chance—just a *chance*, mind you—that I may be close to solving the mystery of why your great-aunt wrote that letter to Pierre's grandfather."

Lisa was eager to hear more, but instead, Nancy described her two friends' reaction on hearing about the old gowns in the attic, and then asked if they might see them.

"By all means, Nancy! You and Bess and George must come over this afternoon," Lisa said.

"I know your father isn't very happy to have me intrude, so if you'd rather not . . ." Nancy left the rest of the sentence unspoken.

"Don't give it another thought," Lisa said firmly. "That no longer bothers me. It happens my father is at home this afternoon, but the invitation still stands. Come on over!"

Nancy chuckled as she put the receiver back on its hook, feeling in better spirits than she had a few minutes ago. It certainly sounded as if changes were taking place in the Thorpe household!

When the three girls arrived at Lisa's place, they were greeted politely but coldly by Mr. Thorpe. He retreated to his study as Lisa came into the hall. She smiled happily at Bess and Nancy and showed equal pleasure in meeting George.

"Could we show my cousin that portrait of Paul and Yvette Duval, Lisa?" Bess asked, trying to contain her excitement.

"Of course . . . especially since she's the lady who wore the gowns!"

After they had viewed the portrait, Lisa led the way to the attic staircase.

Even on a bright afternoon, it was spooky up there, and Bess shivered expectantly. But when the light was turned on and the trunk opened, she forgot her apprehension in her delight over the rich clothes.

When George and Bess exclaimed over the brocades and satins and fine muslins, Nancy lifted out the rough peasant dress. As she did so, its hem brushed against the metal edge of the trunk and she heard a slight clink.

Nancy gave a start, them checked for the cause of the sound. *Something was sewn into the hem of the dress!*

19

The Eyes Have It!

"What's the matter, Nancy?" said Lisa, noticing the startled expression on her face.

"I may be wrong," the teenager said, choking back a surge of excitement, "but something tells me I've just stumbled on a clue!"

The other girls' eyes widened as Nancy showed them a bulge in the hem of the old gown. By fingering it, they could see and feel that the hidden object was oval-shaped and slightly larger than a half-dollar.

"Quick! Someone open the hem and let's see what's in there!" George exclaimed.

"Wait a sec! I'll get some embroidery scissors!" Lisa scampered downstairs and soon returned with the scissors. As the other three watched breathlessly, she cut open the hem and fished out the object which had been concealed inside.

It was a miniature portrait, beautifully enameled on ivory, of a little boy about four or five years old!

All four girls studied the miniature with avid interest as Lisa held it up to the light.

"What a darling little boy!" Bess gushed.

"Gosh! I'll bet that's really valuable!" her cousin added. The portrait was bordered all around the edge with tiny seed pearls.

But Lisa and Nancy were more intrigued by the child's features and general facial appearance.

Lisa looked up tensely.

"Does that little boy remind you of anyone, Nancy?" she asked in a slightly hushed voice.

"Indeed he does!" Nancy replied with a twinkle.

"Whom? . . . Tell me, please!"

"The same person he reminds *you* of, I'll bet . . . *Pierre Michaud!*"

"Right!" Lisa declared emphatically.

The more they studied the miniature portrait, the more they were struck by the resemblance. Despite the difference in ages, and the little boy's softer, more babyish features, the likeness was unmistakeable!

181

The boy even had a dimple in his chin, which as he grew older would doubtless have come to look very much like Pierre's strong, cleft lower jaw.

"He's a darling!" Bess repeated. "I especially like those big, dark eyes, don't you, George? They're so wide-set and . . . sort of *slanty!*"

"I'll have to admit, he's quite a charmer," agreed George, for once not inclined to make fun of her cousin's romantic notions. "If your friend Pierre looks anything like this, Lisa, he must be something special."

"Oh, he is—believe me!" Lisa giggled.

But Nancy was silent and reflective. Bess's remark had started a sudden train of thought, reminding her of the other portrait they had just seen.

"Would you people come downstairs again for a moment?" the young detective said abruptly. "There's something I'd like to show you."

"Okay, but what?" George Fayne inquired.

"I'd rather not say anything just yet and let you judge for yourselves. Lisa, bring the miniature, will you please?"

The others followed, their curiosity piqued by Nancy's words and manner as she led the way back down to the first-floor hall, where the double portrait of Paul and Yvette Duval was hanging on the wall near the sun room.

"Bess," she said, "does either of these people have eyes like the little boy's in the miniature?"

Bess squealed in excitement and pointed to Yvette. "Of course! *She* does! . . . Oh, Nancy! How smart of you to notice!"

George concurred, after glancing back and forth from the miniature to the oil portrait. "You're right, Nancy. They certainly do have the same look across the eyes!"

"And so," the young detective added significantly, "does Pierre Michaud!"

In the startled silence that followed, Lisa Thorpe looked flabbergasted and slightly dismayed. "You're right, Nancy! But, good grief, are you implying that Pierre may be a blood relative of mine?"

Nancy laughed. "Don't worry, he wouldn't be a close enough one to prevent your marriage, if that's what you're wondering. Not after your ancestors have been living on opposite sides of the ocean for almost two centuries!"

Lisa heaved a little sigh of relief and joined in the other girls' laughter at Nancy's reply. But then her mood turned serious.

"You know, this is really quite an important discovery. I think we should tell my father."

Norton Thorpe was in his den, going over a sheaf of business papers at his beautiful fruitwood desk. After announcing herself with a knock, Lisa entered with her friends and related the startling news.

Her father was flushed and angry and scoffed at her revelation. He obviously found the idea that Pierre Michaud was in any way related to his wife's side of the family highly upsetting. But after careful scrutiny of the miniature, it was clear that he, too, could see an unmistakable likeness between the young Frenchman and the boy in the portrait—especially in view of Louise Duval's mysterious letter to Pierre's grandfather.

"Confound it, this is the worst news I've heard in a long time!" he exploded huffily. "If you'll forgive my bluntness, Miss Drew, you've been a most disturbing influence in this house!"

Getting up from his desk, the heavyset businessman paced irritably about the room. "Mind you," he added with a scowl at Nancy, "I'm still not totally convinced that French upstart has any connection with the Duval family!"

Nancy decided that her best tactic was a simple, direct question. "Mr. Thorpe, why are you so dead set against Pierre Michaud?" she asked quietly. "Other people seem to find him perfectly decent and likeable. Do you know something about him that the rest of us don't?"

Norton Thorpe stopped pacing abruptly and glared at the young detective. "Since you ask me, Miss Drew, I see no reason to beat around the bush. The answer is *yes*! I do know something about Michaud that you don't know—and let me add, it's nothing to his credit!"

He related that soon after Pierre's first visit to the Thorpe home, a French lawyer had come to his office to warn him that the young inventor was an unscrupulous swindler and con artist.

"What was this French lawyer's name, Mr. Thorpe?" asked Nancy.

"Grison. Henri Grison. I probably still have his business card." Taking a folder wallet from his inside coat pocket, Mr. Thorpe fingered through its contents and plucked out a card, which he handed to Nancy.

She glanced at it and smiled. "It happens this same person came to see my father, who's also a lawyer," she told Thorpe. "Dad took the trouble to check him out through his own legal correspondents in France. They told him the identification is false—there's no such lawyer at this address or anywhere else in Paris. The only con artist is this so-called Henri Grison himself."

Norton Thorpe was clearly taken aback by Nancy's unexpected reply. But after humming and hawing for a moment, he seemed to accept what she had just told him. "Hmph, well, I must admit this puts matters in a somewhat different light," he conceded.

Lisa was delighted by this sudden turn of

events. "Nancy, you're a wonder!" she exclaimed, giving the girl a quick hug.

With Mr. Thorpe's permission, Nancy now phoned Pierre at his workshop and asked him to come and join them. The young Frenchman not only did so promptly, but brought exciting news of his own.

"Just before you called, Nancy, I had a visit from that representative of the National Computer Company," Pierre reported. "His firm's research and development department have already been over the test data I sent them. And now that he's seen how my computer memory operates, his company's ready to negotiate a licensing contract to produce my invention!"

The contract, Pierre added, would bring him huge sums in royalties every year.

This news was evidently all that was needed to bring about a further drastic change in Norton Thorpe's attitude toward the young inventor. "Well, my boy, it seems congratulations are in order," he beamed, offering Pierre a firm handshake. "It would appear that you're headed for a highly successful industrial career!"

The excited reaction to Pierre's announcement had barely died down when Nancy returned to the subject of the original mystery. "I believe I now know why Miss Duval sent that letter to your grandfather, Pierre," the teenage detective said. "Unfortunately, other people know too, and I think that's why such unpleasant things have been happening to both of us since I began investigating this case."

"Don't keep us in suspense, Nancy!" Bess begged. "Clue us in on the mystery!"

But the pretty young sleuth smiled and shook her head. "Not yet. Before I make any brash statements, I want proof—and I think I know where to look for it."

Nancy was hoping that Professor Crawford's desk in the old mill near Peachtown might still hold some records or notes of the historical research he had done for Louise Duval. If so, this material could either confirm or disprove her theory.

After explaining all this to the others, she pointed out that much of the professor's information had probably come from French sources. Therefore Pierre might be able to help her translate and sort through such material more quickly.

"Would you be willing to come with me?" she asked him.

"Of course, Nancy. When would you like to go?"

"Peachtown's quite a drive from here. So the sooner we leave, the sooner we'll be back."

Pierre chuckled and shrugged. "In that case, let us leave *tout de suite!*"

The two started out in hopeful high spirits. But an annoying delay was in store. Halfway to Peachtown, Nancy's car overheated and stalled. After it had been towed to the nearest repair garage, the trouble was traced to a broken water pump, and a new one had to be sent for. While this was being put in, Nancy and Pierre ate an early dinner of hamburgers and french fries at a roadside drive-in. It was after dark when they reached their destination.

The old mill, with its water wheel and mill-race, was located in a rural setting which might have been delightful to explore on a sunny summer afternoon. But now, as they pulled up outside the old building, with a chill night wind rustling the autumn leaves, a gloomy and forbidding atmosphere pervaded the scene.

Nancy shivered as they got out of the car. "Let's hope this doesn't take too long," she murmured to Pierre.

After opening the mill door with the key that Mrs. Grale had lent her, they mounted a rickety wooden staircase which spiraled upward to a loftlike room above the mill's machinery and grindstones.

The room, which was dusty and evidently seldom used, had been fitted out into a com-

fortable den and study. Nancy uttered a little cry of excitement as she saw an old desk in one corner near a window. Her excitement increased when, after checking two drawers, she came upon a well-filled loose-leaf binder labeled *Report to Louise Duval*.

"Look!" she cried jubilantly, holding it up to show Pierre. "This should give us all the answers!"

The young Frenchman beamed a look of admiration at the teenager. "You are indeed an amazing detective, Nancy! And have you already guessed the contents of that report?"

Nancy nodded as she glanced through its opening pages. "I think I can guess the gist of it, anyhow, though I won't know for sure until I read all of this. If my theory's right, Pierre, you're *the present Count d'Auvergne!*"

His jaw dropped open in astonishment. "Are you saying I am a . . . a French nobleman?"

"Yes, that's exactly what I'm saying. And, hopefully, this report by Professor Crawford should supply the proof."

"You're quite right, my dear Miss Drew," boomed a familiar voice. "Which, I'm afraid, spells bad news for both of you!"

The two young people whirled in surprise and saw that a burly figure had just burst into the room. He was Pierre's financial backer, Mr.

Varney! Beside him stood a short, muscular, apelike man clad in a checked suit and green turtleneck with a cap pulled jauntily low over one eye. He was carrying something in his hand.

"Mr. Varney!" Pierre exclaimed. "How did you get here?"

"No problem, mon *ami*." With a chuckle, Varney gestured to his apelike companion. "My *garçon* here, Louie Bousha, managed to slip into the repair garage where Miss Drew's car was being fixed after its downhill crash in the storm. While the mechanic was busy in the front of the shop, he slipped an electronic beeper under its rear bumper, so that we had simply to follow your radio signal. A most convenient way of trailing you without being seen!"

"Very well," Nancy said, trying to appear cool. "So you've followed us here, and you just heard me tell Pierre about Professor Crawford's report. What good will it do you?"

"It will enable me to get rid of you both, Miss Drew, before you cause me any more trouble. Louie, do you have the anesthetic ready?"

"Right here in this can!" The apelike man grinned, slipping a mask over his nose and mouth. "One whiff will put them out fast!"

Varney turned back to face Nancy and Pierre. "You will then be taken outside and put in Miss

Drew's car, with the engine running and all doors and windows closed. Louie, who is an excellent mechanic, will make sure there is an exhaust leak into the passenger compartment. You can imagine, I am sure, what will be the state of your health after inhaling those deadly fumes!"

20

History Lesson

Nancy caught her breath in dismay, but tried not to let her fear show in her eyes. "Don't be ridiculous," she retorted. "You can't possibly get away with such a crazy scheme!

"But why not, Miss Drew?" Varney's lips curved in a mocking smile. "A wind is blowing, the night is getting colder. And there is certainly no heat in this old mill. So naturally, if the two of you should decide to sit and talk in your car, you would let the engine run and turn on the heater in order to keep warm. Unfortunately, it will appear that you sat there chatting too long, with the windows closed, unaware of the dangerous exhaust leak. *Enfin*, the unhappy result can only be called an accident, *n'est-ce pas?*" The financier broke off with a harsh laugh.

Pierre Michaud stared at him in angry bewilderment. "What is all this you are saying, Varney? Before tonight, you have helped me and supported my work! But now you come here acting like an enemy! Like a criminal who wishes to get rid of me and my friend, Nancy Drew! Have you lost your mind, monsieur? And why," Pierre added, frowning intently, "are you now speaking like a Frenchman, instead of an American?"

"Because he is a Frenchman," said Nancy. "Don't ask me why he's able to speak English so well, or how he managed to pass himself off as an American so successfully. But I'll bet he followed you over to this country from France, Pierre—and for a very good reason!"

"For what reason?" Pierre shot a puzzled glance at the girl. "I do not understand, Nancy . . ."

"To stop you from becoming the Count d'Auvergne. Am I right—*Monsieur Vernet?*"

The financier eyed her coldly. "Perhaps you would care to explain why you call me by that name, Miss Drew?"

"Certainly! Why not? When I glanced through the opening pages of Professor Crawford's report just now, I noticed that Yvette Duval's *first* married name was Yvette Vernet. And I strongly suspect that you belong to the same family as her first husband, which means your real name is also probably Vernet. *N'est-ce pas, monsieur?*"

This time it was Nancy who spoke in a mocking tone. She was trying to keep the conversation going, in the desperate hope that she or Pierre could find some way to overtake their captors.

The man who called himself Varney chuckled again. "You are even smarter than I thought, my dear Miss Drew. Which makes it clearer than ever that I must get rid of you both!"

No doubt Pierre would have been more confused than ever by this latest exchange of remarks, had he been listening. But his attention had just wandered. While Nancy and Varney were speaking, he noticed that both crooks had their eyes focused on the girl detective. Cautiously, he reached out and took a firm grip on the desk chair . . . and suddenly hurled it at the burly financier!

The chair sent Varney toppling sideways against his apelike henchman! Louie Bousha too went down!

Before the crooks could recover, Pierre pounced on them, lashing out furiously with his fists as they struggled to their feet!

Bousha was still clutching the deadly canister. Nancy sent it flying from his hand with a swift kick in the wrist.

Just then, footsteps came pounding up the stairs and another man rushed into the room. He was dark-haired and tough-looking. Nancy's heart sank as she recognized him as her swarthy shadow. But a moment later, her dismay changed to excited relief. He was helping Pierre fight Varney and Louie Bousha!

There were tense moments as the struggle surged back and forth across the room. Then Nancy suddenly saw her chance. Grasping the overturned chair which Pierre had thrown, she gave it a hard shove. It slid across the floor, banging into Varney's left ankle. Startled, he lost his balance, and a second later a hard punch by Pierre knocked him sprawling!

The fight was soon over. Battered and subdued, with their hands tied behind them, the two crooks glared at the victors. Pierre, who was still panting from his exertions but also grinning in triumph, gave Nancy a quick hug and kiss.

"Forgive the liberty, *ma chérie*, but without your help, we might never have won!

Nancy smiled and squeezed his hand, then turned to their swarthy ally. "I think we both owe this gentleman a vote of thanks, Pierre. His name is André Freneau. If you'll remember, we saw him outside the restaurant on that day you and I met in my father's office. Perhaps now he'll tell us how he came into this case."

Freneau was startled to learn that Nancy already knew his name. He took out his passport and official identification to show the two Americans. "As you see, Mademoiselle Drew, I am a French private detective," he said, then smiled and bowed and held out his hand. "But may I offer my congratulations to one who is obviously a much better detective than I am ever likely to be!"

Both Nancy and Pierre shook his hand warmly.

"May I also apologize for any trouble I may have caused," Freneau went on, "especially on that night in front of your house, Mademoiselle Drew. You see, I trailed your friend here, Pierre Michaud, and also that fellow Vernet, over to this country from France. I knew Vernet was a scoundrel, so when it appeared that he and Pierre Michaud were working together, I wrongly concluded that all three of you were engaged in some criminal scheme."

Pierre's dark eyes kindled with interest on hearing Freneau mention Vernet-alias-Varney. "What can you tell us about him, monsieur?" he asked.

The French detective smiled grimly. "I feel quite sure this shrewd young lady already knows the most important fact about his identity. Am I correct, Mademoiselle Drew?"

Nancy smiled back, then glanced at the

scowling face of Vernet. "Since he's tried so hard to keep Pierre from discovering his true birthright, I'm almost certain he himself must be the former claimant to the title."

Freneau smiled approvingly. "Correct, mademoiselle. He is Ètienne Vernet, and up until tonight, he has been able to call himself the Comte d'Auvergne!"

Later, after the two crooks had been turned over to the state police, Nancy and Pierre returned to the Thorpes' house, with André Freneau as an additional guest. Bess and George were also on hand to witness the outcome of the case.

By this time, Nancy had been able to read through Professor Crawford's report. So when the group clamored to hear her solution to the mystery, she was able to fill in the previously missing details.

"Your ancestress, Yvette Duval," Nancy told Lisa, "was originally married to a French nobleman—Philippe Vernet, who held the title of Comte d'Auvergne. Their son was that little boy shown on the miniature. Unfortunately, France was plunged into revolution just about that time, and the royal government was so hated that almost every member of the nobility that the mob could lay hands on was put to death. So Yvette and her husband made plans to flee across the Channel to England to save their lives."

Yvette's sister Charlotte, the teenage sleuth explained, had previously married an Englishman and was already living in that country.

"I knew from Charlotte's letter," Nancy went on, "that Yvette had had to leave some 'precious treasure' behind in France. Then when we found the miniature, I began to wonder if that little boy on it might have been her lost treasure. After all, what could be more precious to any mother than her child? And when we noticed the family resemblance between that little boy and Pierre, the whole jigsaw puzzle began to fit together."

"But wait!" Bess Marvin spoke up in a puzzled voice. "Why on earth did she hide that beautiful miniature away in a shabby old gown?"

Nancy smiled. "Because that shabby old gown was the disguise she wore during her escape from France. The Vernets didn't dare risk their son's life—there was too much risk of being caught. So they left him behind in the care of a kind-hearted village notary and his wife, named Michaud. Even the possession of such a valuable object as that miniature might have given the couple away as aristocrats. That's why Yvette sewed it in the hem of her gown—to keep it from being discovered, and also, of course, so she could have that cherished picture of her little boy to remember him by until she could see him again."

Nancy's face saddened as she described the tragic events that followed.

"Before they could escape from France, Philippe was recognized as a nobleman and carted off to the guillotine in Paris. Yvette, however, managed to avoid capture, thanks to her disguise as a peasant girl, and boarded a ship at Calais that took her across the Channel. But as a result of her terrifying ordeal, she suffered a loss of memory and landed in England in a state of total amnesia."

Luckily, Nancy added, her sister Charlotte identified and took care of the unhappy young woman. Eventually Yvette regained most of her memory and married Paul Duval, a banker of mixed Anglo-French parentage. But ever afterward, she preferred never to think or talk about the terrible circumstances that had cost her first husband his life.

Lisa exclaimed softly, "So that's why her story was never passed down in the family, from generation to generation!"

Nancy nodded thoughtfully. "You'll be interested to know, too, that according to Professor Crawford's papers, Paul Duval was a widower with one son when he married Yvette.

It was that son who carried on the Duval name. Only daughters were born to Yvette and Paul after their marriage, and I suspect they may have learned about her escape from France during the Reign of Terror. But the details probably soon got blurred and were forgotten. I guess most of us never bother to ask our parents and grandparents much about the past until it's too late.

"Because of the disturbed conditions in France due to the Revolution and the Napoleonic wars that followed, Yvette never recovered her lost child. The Michauds, who had long since moved from their native village, brought up the little boy as their own son.

"The only other relic of the past was the portrait of Yvette's first husband. Apparently her sister Charlotte was somehow able to retrieve this from the Comte's chateau and have it smuggled to England, soon after Yvette's flight to freedom. Perhaps seeing it helped Yvette recover her memory," Nancy mused.

"Since nothing was known about their little son's fate, a cousin of the count claimed his chateau and estate and became accepted as the new Comte d'Auvergne. Like other nobles who swore allegiance to the Revolutionary government, he was allowed to keep his title.

"By the time the River Heights art museum

opened a century later, the Duval family did not even know whom the oil portrait of Philippe Vernet represented. So they donated it to the museum.

"I suppose the whole story might never have come to light," Nancy told her audience, "if one day the curator hadn't had the picture taken down and placed in storage. Miss Louise Duval was so annoyed that she called in an art expert to prove the picture was valuable. It was through him that she learned the painting was a portrait of the Comte d'Auvergne . . . which in turn made her realize her family might be descended from French nobility.

"Miss Duval," Nancy went on, "then hired Professor Crawford to trace her family's history and try to prove her exciting secret hunch. His summer's research in England and France uncovered the fact that Pierre's Grandfather Michaud was a direct descendent of the count and countess's lost little son. This made him— and later Pierre—the true present-day Count d'Auvergne and therefore the rightful inheritor of the Chateau d'Auvergne and all its surrounding vast estate.

"Unfortunately, Ètienne Vernet, like his forefathers, had grown used to being the count and enjoying the wealth that went with the count's estate. He had no intention of giving up the title.

"From what Monsieur Freneau told us," said Nancy, "we know now that Vernet did away with a French private detective whom the professor had hired to gather evidence in the case.

"Under grilling by the state police," Nancy added, "Vernet also admitted that he had flown to this country and tried to run down Miss Duval with a car in order to stop her from pursuing her investigation.

"His effort, in fact, succeeded. Louise Duval succumbed to a heart attack, and as a result, Professor Crawford simply left his unfinished report lying in his desk drawer.

"At the time of the professor's research, Etienne Vernet was twenty-six years old. From that point on, he kept careful tab on the Michauds in order to thwart any future attempt they might make to claim the title.

"After reading a French newspaper interview with Pierre Michaud, the false count went into action. The interview told how Pierre was coming to America to develop and market his computer device, and also to find out why Louise Duval had written the mysterious letter to his grandfather thirty years ago.

"Vernet—who had been educated in the

United States and spoke English fluently—posed as 'Mr. Varney' in order to keep in touch with Pierre's activities, and also to obstruct and discredit him in any way possible. This included starting the fire in his workshop, planting the booby trap, and spreading malicious lies about him while posing as a French lawyer.

"With the help of his stooge, Louie Bousha, Vernet also tried to steal the original count's portrait from the museum and scare me off the case by chasing me in a red car and tampering with my power steering."

"You told us that red car didn't seem to have any driver, Nancy," George Fayne spoke up. "How did the big crook manage that trick?"

"Actually it was his hired hand, Louie Bousha, who was at the wheel," the young detective replied, "and he wore a black hood which made him almost impossible to see in the darkness."

"Yikes!" George exclaimed. "Pretty neat!"

"It was also Bousha who broke into your attic," Nancy told Lisa. "That was because Varney had heard from Pierre that you'd invited me to come over the next day and search your great-aunt's effects. But we spoiled their plan when you phoned and asked me to come over that same night."

"What a lucky break!" exclaimed Lisa. "Otherwise they might have found the ring and the miniature before we did!"

Nancy then invited the French detective, André Freneau, to tell his story. He revealed that it was his father who had been hired by Professor Crawford to help investigate the background of the Michaud family and the rightful ownership of the d'Auvergne estate, and who had later been done away with by Ètienne Vernet.

"I always suspected my father's death was due to foul play," Freneau told his circle of listeners. "When I learned that Pierre Michaud and Vernet were both coming to this country, I at first suspected they were engaged in some new criminal plot. Thanks to Mademoiselle Drew, however, I eventually learned which one was the real criminal."

Nancy added that following Vernet's arrest, she had also found out that during his trip to America thirty years ago, he had paid the then law clerk Maxwell Fleen for information about his firm's client, Miss Louise Duval.

Chubby Bess Marvin looked shocked on hearing this. "If Fleen's a lawyer now," she said indignantly, "shouldn't he be disbarred from practice for doing such a thing?"

"That's a matter I intend to take up with my father," Nancy replied discreetly.

The evening ended on an especially happy note when Pierre Michaud proudly announced that Lisa Thorpe had accepted his proposal of marriage.

When the applause and excitement had subsided enough for him to be heard, he turned with a somewhat uncertain smile to Mr. Thorpe and added, "I trust her father will not object to our engagement?"

"He'd better not!" Lisa said, only half jokingly and with a new firmness in her voice.

Norton Thorpe clapped the young Frenchman on the shoulder and, with a hearty smile, shook his hand. "My dear chap! How could I possibly object to my daughter becoming not only the new Countess d'Auvergne but also the wife of an up-and-coming electronics genius!" Lisa, her eyes moist with tears of joy, not only because of her future marriage but also because of her restored relationship with her father, threw her arms around Nancy in a warm embrace exclaiming: "Oh, Nancy, none of this could ever have happened if you hadn't worked so hard to solve the mystery."

For a moment, the girl detective wondered how difficult her next case would be. She did not expect an answer so soon when she found "The Broken Anchor."

"How can we ever thank you?" Lisa asked.

"You already have," Nancy said, blinking her eyes. "That look of happiness on your face is my greatest reward."

NANCY DREW MYSTERY STORIES®
by Carolyn Keene

You will also enjoy

THE LINDA CRAIG® SERIES
by Ann Sheldon